THE UNAFFECTED EARL

LANDING A LORD

SUZANNA MEDEIROS

Copyright © 2018 by Saozinha Medeiros

THE UNAFFECTED EARL
First Digital Edition: September 2018
First Print Edition: September 2018
Cover design © Kim Killion, The Killion Group, Inc.
Edited by Victory Editing
ebook ISBN: 9781988223087
Paperback ISBN: 9781988223094

This is a work of fiction. Names, characters, places, and incidents either
are the product of the author's imagination or are used fictitiously, and
any resemblance to actual persons, living or dead, business
establishments, events, or locales is entirely coincidental.

All rights reserved. Except as permitted under the U.S. Copyright Act of
1976, no part of this publication may be reproduced, stored in or
introduced into a retrieval system, or transmitted, in any form, or by any
means (electronic, mechanical, photocopying, recording, or otherwise),
without the prior written permission of the author.

*To everyone who has been waiting so patiently for this book.
I hope you enjoy reading it as much as I enjoyed writing it.*

THE UNAFFECTED EARL

They call him the Unaffected Earl…
Many seek his favor, men and women alike, but few glimpse what lies beneath the Earl of Brantford's aloof exterior.

She was the woman everyone wanted…
Rose Hardwick was the most sought-after debutante in London until scandal touched her family and made her a social pariah.

He alone has the power to help her…
Rose is determined to prove her father innocent of the crime of treason, but first she must convince the Unaffected Earl to help her. When circumstances force them closer together, will she be able to thaw the ice that encases his heart?

To learn about Suzanna Medeiros's future books, you can sign up for her new release newsletter at https://www.suzannamedeiros.com/newsletter

CHAPTER 1

June 1807

THE EARL OF BRANTFORD left the shadows and approached the dark-haired man who waited outside the cell housing the most recent prisoner of the Tower of London. He gave a curt nod to the guard who also stood outside the cell. The guard gave no indication he'd seen Brantford's silent command, but he moved away. Not far enough that anyone could accuse him of shirking his duty, but the distance ensured Brantford had privacy for this conversation.

He got straight to the point. "You need to keep her away from here."

The Earl of Kerrick showed no hint of surprise at seeing him. "I cannot control what Rose Hardwick chooses to do. I couldn't when everyone expected us to wed, and I certainly can't now that she's given me my freedom. But I can keep her safe. For everything she's sacrificed to bring Catherine and me together, it's the least I owe her."

Brantford tamped down the irritation that sparked within him at the reminder of the other man's former relationship with Rose. It had never been more than a courtship—one Brantford himself had ordered Kerrick to pursue—but the casual reference to their short-lived betrothal served as an unwelcome reminder that a small part of him had wanted to perform that particular duty.

"If you wish to keep her safe, you'll ensure she doesn't repeat today's visit. Coming here makes her a target."

Kerrick knew he spoke the truth. Brantford could see it in the tightening of his jaw. Neither of them believed that Rose's father had acted alone. And if the man they suspected of actually committing the treasonous acts to which Worthington had confessed even suspected he'd shared any information with his daughter, he wouldn't hesitate to silence her forever.

"What would you have me do? Restrain her and force her to stay away? Rose's mother only agreed to allow her to remain with Overlea when she left London because of her friendship with Catherine. Being under the protection of a marquess was more than the poor woman could have hoped for after Rose ended her betrothal to me. But Overlea isn't about to keep her locked in his home. He'd bring her to the Tower himself, but we all know I owe her at least this much. After the turmoil of the past few days and the way everyone has turned their back on her, I'm not about to keep her from seeing her father."

Brantford wanted to insist he do just that—lock Rose Hardwick in her bedroom and post someone outside her window, if need be, to keep her safe. But knowing that would never happen, his thoughts turned to the next best course of action.

It was obvious that Lord Worthington had confessed to treason to protect his wife and daughter. It wouldn't take much effort to convince the man that the best way to keep his daughter safe would be to refuse to see her. After being turned away a few times, Rose would eventually stop visiting. Hopefully that would happen before she attracted further attention. Damn her stubborn hide —she would be safe now if she'd fled London with her mother.

Brantford turned to leave, deciding it would be best to return later, when he wouldn't be in danger of seeing the woman who was occupying far too much of his thoughts of late. So of course the door to the cell swung open just then and Rose Hardwick exited the room where her father was being held. Her head was bowed, but despite the defeat evident in her posture, he was struck, as always, by her beauty. It had been almost one week since he'd last seen her, when she'd arrived at Kerrick's town house to inform him she'd taken steps to set him free from his promise to wed her. It had been a betrothal neither wanted, but with Kerrick's name, Rose would have had some protection from the cruel tongues that even now ripped apart her family's reputation.

Brantford had hoped never to see her again.

Instead of her normal curls, she wore her reddish-brown hair tightly bound. But that wasn't the only change in her appearance. When she lifted her face to look at Kerrick, Brantford could see the signs of strain the past few days had wrought. The dark shadows under her eyes were new. She'd attempted to conceal them with powder, no doubt in an attempt to keep her father from worrying about her, but no amount of cosmetics could hide them completely. And there was a tightness to her features, an air of fragility about her that made him want to take her into his arms and protect her from the world. He wouldn't, of course, and it rankled that this woman could bring out such emotion in him. Emotions were a sign of weakness, and he would do nothing to betray himself. He'd learned that lesson at his father's knee while still a lad.

When Kerrick offered her his arm, she gave him a weary smile before taking it. Brantford knew for a fact that there was nothing untoward between the two of them, but he couldn't stop the annoyance that flared to life as he watched them standing together.

She noticed him then. She must have assumed he was the guard when she'd first exited her father's prison, but when she recognized him, her blue eyes hardened and her delectable bow of a mouth firmed into a straight line.

For some reason Rose had gone from seeming indifference toward him to an active dislike, and he couldn't fathom why. He'd barely spoken to her, making sure to keep his distance whenever they happened to attend the same social events. He couldn't account for her sudden hostility, but he wouldn't allow it to affect him.

"Miss Hardwick," he said, inclining his head by way of greeting. Given the grim nature of her visit, there wasn't anything he could say to her beyond that. He'd called upon her mother the day before, catching her just before she'd quit London, but the woman hadn't been able to tell him anything. Rose had already taken up residence at the Overlea town house, a fact that suited him. If Lady Worthington knew nothing about her husband's actions, it was unlikely that he'd be able to learn anything from their daughter.

Rose turned away but said nothing. There was nothing to say, after all.

He met Kerrick's gaze, sending him a silent command to do whatever he could to keep Rose away. The other man's brows drew together briefly before he led Rose down the hallway.

Never mind. Brantford would handle the matter. He'd allowed others to question Worthington, and their efforts hadn't borne any fruit. He'd also ensure Rose's father would take the necessary steps to keep any further harm from coming to his daughter.

Knowing the guard would do nothing to bar his entry, Brantford approached the cell. Catching Worthington by surprise so soon after his daughter's visit might be an advantage. If the man was affected even half as much as his daughter had been, it might give Brantford the edge he needed to break his silence.

Since Worthington was merely a viscount with only a meager amount of wealth, he hadn't merited one of the more elaborate rooms in the Tower. Rooms that had once housed royalty.

No, this room barely contained the necessities. A small cot in the corner served as a bed, a small screen in another corner hiding the chamber pot. One that hadn't been emptied for some time if the smell that permeated the air was any indication. The air hung heavy and damp. There were several small windows high along one wall, but the daylight that entered did little to alleviate the gloom of the cell.

He'd been in many such cells during his time working for the Home Office, and none of those visits had ever affected him. After all, one gave up all right to luxury and comfort when they committed treason. But today, knowing that Rose had been in that room mere moments before, knowing that she'd looked upon the defeated man hunched over on the edge of the small cot, Brantford felt an unaccustomed heaviness in his chest.

Not for the man seated before him but for his daughter who'd been forced to see him that way.

If he had a heart, he supposed he would have felt sorry for Worthington as well. Instead, all he could summon was annoyance. And if he was being honest with himself, a hint of anger at what the man had done to his family.

When all this had started, Brantford had hoped the rumblings his agents had uncovered about Worthington

6

selling English secrets to the French would come to naught. It had been a vain hope, but he'd wanted to find something—anything—that would lead to another explanation. But now that Worthington had confessed, that hope was gone.

Worthington hadn't heard him enter, his demeanor that of a man who was deep in thought. Brantford crossed the room and lowered himself into the chair Rose had no doubt been sitting in during her visit, breaking into the man's reverie with a suddenness that made Worthington jump.

Worthington's gaze hardened when he realized Rose hadn't returned to see him. It appeared the man's defenses hadn't been shattered after all by his daughter's visit.

Brantford started on his questioning, but he already knew he would learn nothing new. He wouldn't leave this room, however, until he'd extracted Worthington's promise to turn away any future visits from his daughter.

CHAPTER 2

*R*OSE APPRECIATED THE FACT that Lord
Kerrick didn't try to engage in small talk
during their return carriage ride. There was nothing to
say, after all.

Her father had refused to discuss what had
happened. She knew he wasn't guilty of treason, could
feel it in her heart with a certainty that was unshakable.
But he seemed resigned to accept what would happen to
him because of his confession, his concern solely for
Rose and her mother. When her mother left town mere
days after her father had been taken to the Tower of
London, she'd tried to insist that Rose leave with her. If
her friend Catherine Evans hadn't invited her to stay
with her family—extending, by default, the protection
of her brother-in-law, the Marquess of Overlea—she
might never have seen her father again.

She'd already been frustrated that her father refused
to speak about why he would confess to a crime he

hadn't committed. Finding the Earl of Brantford outside her father's cell afterward had been more than she could bear. The irony was not lost on her that she'd spent most of the season trying, unsuccessfully, to capture his interest. Aside from the musicale her parents had hosted, when Brantford had spoken to her for the briefest of moments, he'd barely glanced in her direction all season.

Of all the times when fate could have thrown the two of them together, it was cruel that she would choose to do so now after Rose's family had been thoroughly ruined. Not that Brantford had ever shown the slightest inclination that he was interested in her romantically. She'd always held out a small ray of hope where he was concerned, but now she had to face reality. The Earl of Brantford would never align himself with the daughter of a confessed traitor.

When they reached the Overlea town house, Kerrick saw her to the door.

"Are you not coming inside?" she asked when he made no move to open the door.

He shook his head. "I have things I need to attend to today. But please tell Catherine that I will be by later this afternoon to see her. And you too, of course."

Rose hesitated a moment before speaking the words that would acknowledge the task they'd been on that morning. Foolish, really, since they both knew what had happened. Lord Kerrick had been with her every step of the way, after all. Still, it was difficult to talk about it.

"Thank you for accompanying me today."

"It's the very least I can do. I owe you a debt I can never repay."

Rose managed a ghost of a smile. "Nonsense. You and I were never suited. It was the wish of our parents that we wed, but your heart lies elsewhere. I knew that from the start." *As does mine*, she thought, trying to ignore the bitterness that threatened to overwhelm her. Dwelling on unrequited feelings that could never lead anywhere was pointless.

"What do you plan to do now?"

Kerrick's question surprised her. "I intend to see my father again tomorrow, of course."

"Are you sure you want to put yourself through that strain?"

"Of course. I won't abandon him now." She also needed to know why her father would confess to a crime he hadn't committed. Would it even matter though? Could someone ever take back such a confession? In all likelihood, he'd committed himself to the hangman's noose the moment those words had left his lips.

She shook her head to clear it of the fatalistic thoughts. She refused to consider the possibility that there was nothing she could do to help her father. She would be there for him just as he had always been there for her over the years.

"If you can't accompany me, I'll understand. I'll take a maid with me tomorrow." She started to turn away, but his next words stopped her.

"I'll be here tomorrow at the same time, never worry. You will not be going to the Tower alone."

Rose couldn't summon the words to thank him, so instead she nodded in reply. Logic told her that he'd only spoken out of concern for her well-being, but she couldn't quite forgive him for thinking she would turn away from her father. She'd be past her annoyance tomorrow. Her armor would be back in place then, but at that moment she was too emotionally battered to summon the energy required to act her normal, upbeat self.

She made her way inside without another word. Finding the entrance hall empty, she breathed a sigh of relief. She hadn't missed the pitying looks the household staff had directed her way since her arrival two days before. She who, one week before, had been the most sought-after debutante in all of London.

She hesitated outside the drawing room, knowing that Catherine would be waiting for her. After learning that Rose didn't wish to return to the country with her mother, Catherine had invited her to stay with her family and hadn't once pressed her for details. Catherine respected her need for privacy and would understand if she needed some time alone. But despite the temptation to make her way up to her bedchamber, Rose needed answers first.

Her curiosity about Brantford's presence at the Tower had been stirred. As far as she knew, he had no reason for being there. She hadn't realized Brantford was friends with Lord Kerrick until very recently. She couldn't ask Kerrick directly about the other man, but as Kerrick's betrothed, it was possible Catherine might be able to provide answers to her questions. They'd only just become engaged, but Kerrick was a close friend of Catherine's brother-in-law, and she'd known him for some time.

Squaring her shoulders, she entered the drawing room and found her friend curled in an armchair, immersed in a book. Catherine looked up at her entrance and smiled.

Rose couldn't bring herself to return the smile. Instead, she crossed the room and lowered herself onto the settee across from her friend. It took almost everything in her to hold on to her composure after the frustrating visit she'd had with her father.

Catherine closed her book and placed it on her lap, her fingers clutching the spine. That small action warned Rose that her friend was about to break her silence about what had taken place.

"I don't know what to say to you," Catherine said, her voice uncharacteristically soft. "I want to ask how your father is doing—how *you* are feeling after your visit —but I don't wish to intrude if you're not yet ready to talk."

Coming from anyone else, Rose would have hated the sympathy she saw in her friend's eyes, but this was Catherine. They hadn't known each other long, but Catherine had been the only friend to stand by her after her family's fall from grace. More than that, she'd marshaled her whole family to lend their support when no one else would even acknowledge her.

She released a sigh. "You needn't tread so carefully around me."

"I don't want you to think that I'm looking for gossip."

That statement, more than anything else Catherine could have said, brought a smile to Rose's face. "If I believed that was all you wanted from me, I never would have accepted your invitation to stay here."

The slight crease of concern on her friend's forehead cleared. "If you need someone in whom to confide, you know I am here for you."

Rose lifted her shoulder in a slight shrug, the careful movement relaying only a hint of the confusion roiling through her. "Papa seemed concerned about me of course. He hadn't expected to see me. Apparently when Mama visited him, she told him we'd both be returning to the country to stay with her sister."

"That had been her intention. He wouldn't have heard that you were remaining in London before your visit this morning."

"I thought he would be happy that I hadn't abandoned him, but the opposite was true. He insisted that I leave London."

Catherine rose from the armchair, deposited her book on the seat, and moved to sit next to her on the settee. "Your father's concern for you is normal. He doesn't want you to be touched by what is happening to him. You can't fault him for wanting you to be far away from here."

"I won't leave him, and I can't understand why

Mama would. How could she desert him when he needs the support of his family?" Her fists had clenched in her lap, and she took the time to force herself to regulate her breathing and relax her hands before continuing. "You would never abandon anyone in your family if the circumstances were similar... not if you knew them to be innocent."

In reply, Catherine took hold of one of her hands and gave it a slight squeeze before releasing it again.

Rose had to look away. Several seconds passed before she could force down the emotion that threatened to overwhelm her every time she thought of her father and how lost he had appeared in his cold cell. It had been one short week since he was taken away, but he'd aged in that time, and she'd hated to see him so defeated.

When she finally had her emotions in check, she met Catherine's patient gaze. "I wanted to discuss another matter with you. What can you tell me about your soon-to-be husband's friendship with Lord Brantford?"

If Rose hadn't been watching her friend so closely, she might have missed the flicker of unease in Catherine's eyes before she looked away.

"I imagine that Kerrick's circle of acquaintances is quite large."

Catherine's reply wasn't implausible, but the careful manner in which she weighed each word spoke volumes. Her friend was hiding something.

"That is all you can tell me?"

Catherine shrugged. "I know they are on friendly

terms. Kerrick respects Lord Brantford a great deal, but I'm not sure I would call the two of them friends."

"Then how would you characterize their acquaintance?"

Catherine shook her head, and Rose didn't miss the way she fidgeted with her hands, twining them together before catching herself and forcing them to lie flat on her lap.

Rose narrowed her eyes, convinced now more than ever that her friend was deliberately trying to evade her question. "What are you keeping from me?"

Catherine sighed and met her gaze. "Why the sudden interest in Lord Brantford?"

Rose recognized the stalling tactic for what it was. When she didn't want to answer a question, Catherine often turned the subject around so the other person was on the receiving end of the questioning. She contemplated whether to tell her friend the truth.

In the end, she didn't need to. Catherine must have seen it written plainly on her face. It was a small miracle Rose had been able to hide it from her friend for so long.

"It's Brantford," Catherine said with a small gasp of surprise. "He's the man you wouldn't tell me about."

Rose could only nod in reply, the futility of her current situation striking her once again.

"They call him the Unaffected Earl for very good reason. He's not likely to return your affection."

Rose couldn't hold back a small burst of laughter. "I know. It is beyond ridiculous. Of all the men to capture my interest—and heaven knows, many have tried—I have to fixate on the one who has ice water instead of blood running through his veins."

"It has nothing to do with you. He's that way with everyone. When he was at Overlea Manor last year—"

Now it was Rose's turn to gasp and reach for Catherine's hand. She stared at her friend for several moments before finding her voice. "He stayed with you? You never told me that."

"I didn't know it would mean anything to you."

"It does. More than I'd care to admit. Does this mean he is friends with your sister's husband?"

Catherine shook her head. "I don't believe so, no."

Rose released her friend's hand and crossed her arms over her chest, aiming for a levity she was far from feeling as she said, "Don't make me drag the details out of you. I will if I have to."

Catherine smiled, and Rose could almost see the tension leave her slight frame. "He was there at Kerrick's invitation."

Rose scowled at her friend. "Now I know you are toying with me. Tell me everything."

Catherine sighed. "It was a difficult time for my family. Louisa and Nicholas… the marquess… had only been wed for a short time. We all thought he was suffering from the same illness that had taken the lives of his father and his older brother."

"I remember that. Not that he too was ill, but it was so tragic what happened to his family. But surely he's better now?"

"Oh yes," Catherine said with a nod. She hesitated for several seconds before seeming to make up her mind about continuing. "It turned out that he wasn't ill at all. In fact, no one in his family was. We discovered that what they'd all thought was illness was actually the result of someone poisoning them."

Catherine's admission was the last thing Rose expected to hear. Poison? She had heard nothing about that. And to have lost his father and brother to it... She couldn't even begin to fathom what that knowledge had cost the current Marquess of Overlea. From what she'd seen in the short time she'd been living under his roof, he was happily married to Catherine's older sister— their love for one another was evident to everyone who saw them together. Still, it must have cost him dearly to learn his family had died at the hands of another.

"What does this have to do with Brantford?" she asked.

"Kerrick solicited Lord Brantford's assistance in discovering the person responsible. I can't tell you more than that, and I ask that you not share what I've told you. It was a frightening time for everyone, and Nicholas doesn't want his family's hardships turned into idle gossip."

Rose suspected that there was a lot more to the story that Catherine hadn't told her, but she wouldn't press for more details. She, of all people, could understand wanting to keep family matters private. Still, it took an effort of will to keep from insisting Catherine divulge more details. Not that she would, of course. Her friend's sense of honor was one of the reasons Rose felt she could trust her with her own secrets.

"Can you at least tell me why Kerrick called upon Lord Brantford? He's not a magistrate. In what way could he lend assistance?"

"I can't say with any certainty."

The hesitation in Catherine's voice spoke volumes. "Can't or won't? I have a feeling you have a theory."

Catherine shook her head. "Kerrick has tried to dissuade me, but I suspect that Brantford is very well connected in government."

"In what way?" Rose narrowed her eyes, trying to decipher the meaning behind her friend's words.

"Again, I can't say."

Rose was about to insist, but Catherine continued without her needing to ask the question.

"No, really, I have no concrete knowledge from which to form an opinion. As you say, it is only a theory. A sense that Lord Brantford…"

Rose wanted to scream at her friend to stop circling around the subject and speak plainly, but she managed to hold her tongue.

"I don't know what I'm saying. I can't tell you my suspicions because I promised Kerrick I wouldn't spread my beliefs about."

"So you can't tell me why Lord Brantford would be visiting the Tower today? He would have no reason to be there. I don't believe he and Papa have anything more than a passing acquaintance." Rose let out a heavy sigh before continuing. "I've examined the situation from every angle, trying to ascertain a reason for his visit, but can think of nothing. Lord Brantford's presence there makes no sense. I thought that perhaps he might have been there to meet with Lord Kerrick, but surely they would arrange a more appropriate time and place to speak."

She was missing something important about the entire situation. It frustrated her to no end that she couldn't figure out the reason for his presence outside her father's cell that morning.

"I can't divulge my suspicions, but there is nothing stopping me from offering advice."

Rose leaned forward. After the disappointing visit with her father, she wanted to believe Catherine could help her. "I am willing to consider anything. Anything other than the advice to give up on my father and return to the country."

"I wouldn't even attempt to tell you that. You are just as stubborn as I when it comes to trusting your own instincts. If you say that your father is hiding something that might clear him of guilt, I am inclined to believe you."

Emotion swelled in her throat, stealing her voice for several seconds, and she thanked the heavens that had given her such a good friend. "What is your advice?"

Catherine hesitated, and for a moment Rose feared she had changed her mind. She needn't have worried.

"I've already mentioned that Lord Brantford is well connected. The only other thing I can add is that you should arrange to speak to him directly. I suspect there is no one better equipped than he to assist you in proving your father's innocence."

ROSE LAY ACROSS HER BED, staring up at the ceiling as she contemplated her conversation with Catherine.

It was difficult to push aside her embarrassment whenever she thought about Brantford. Her interest in him had always been foolish, and now it was destined to come to nothing. The thought that she would have to appeal to him for assistance was a particularly cruel twist of fate.

It had been a shock to see him at Kerrick's town house when she'd visited him to break their ill-conceived betrothal. She'd tried to push that memory from her mind, especially the way she'd snapped at Brantford, taking out her frustration about her family's current situation on him. But thinking about that day now, she couldn't deny that Catherine might be correct. It was possible that Brantford might be able to help her prove her father's innocence.

He'd asked for leave to call on her mother, and Rose had assured him that she'd convince her mother to speak to him. Only that hadn't happened. Her mother had turned him away, as she had all other callers—gawkers, really, circling around them in an attempt to glean a shred of gossip they could share with their friends. She hadn't known why Brantford had even wanted to speak to her mother, but she'd hoped he could help somehow.

Then her mother had left London, and Rose had forced herself to forget Brantford's cryptic comments on that day. Only now it seemed that had been a mistake.

She covered her face with her hands as she tried to picture how that conversation would unfold. How she'd have to beg him to help her family, all while he looked down at her with that cold impassivity for which he was famous.

The very idea was humiliating. But it was evident she'd have to do it anyway since she had no notion how else to go about clearing her father's name.

She forced herself to sit up and take several deep breaths. Then, squaring her shoulders, she stood and went in search of Catherine. She found her in the garden, fussing with the roses.

Her friend turned to face her when she realized she was no longer alone and smiled. "Did you have a nice rest?"

Rose shook her head. "I couldn't stop thinking about what you said. I've decided to heed your advice. I'm going to ask for Lord Brantford's assistance in proving my father's innocence."

Catherine nodded as though she'd expected her to come to that conclusion all along. "I've been thinking about how to go about this. I think we're going to need to involve Louisa and Kerrick."

Rose had expected that they'd need to involve

Kerrick, but she had to hold back a grimace at the thought of involving Lady Overlea.

"All right. What exactly did you have in mind? I'll admit, I considered marching up to his town house, but his butler would probably toss me out into the street."

"I doubt that," Catherine said. "I'm sure he's used to all manner of individuals turning up to see his employer."

Rose scrunched her nose at that, wondering if many women visited the earl. She forced herself to suppress that thought so she wouldn't drive herself mad with jealousy.

"We could invite him here."

Catherine shook her head. "We don't want to involve Nicholas. He's been like a lion protecting his pride when it comes to us, especially now that my sister is increasing."

"We're talking about a dinner invitation. Surely there's no harm in that."

"No, but given how much the two of them went through when they were first married, Nicholas wants to wrap her up and keep her safe from any harm, whether real or imagined. He's more than happy to have you here, but he doesn't want her involved with anything that might cause her any undue stress."

Rose made her way over to a bench that was situated just outside the garden doors and sat. "I shouldn't be involving you in this."

Catherine sank down beside her. "Nonsense. All we're going to do is pay Lord Brantford a call—you,

SUZANNA MEDEIROS

Kerrick, and me, and Louisa will be there to act as chaperone. It's a bit unorthodox, but it's not like you'll be visiting him alone."

Rose grimaced remembering how she'd marched into Kerrick's town house the day she'd broken their engagement. If anyone had taken note of her arrival, however, they would have seen her depart only a few minutes later. "I'm not sure Lord Kerrick wants you involved in this any more than Lord Overlea wants your sister involved."

Catherine waved a hand in dismissal. "He doesn't really have a choice. He can come with us or he can hear about it after the fact. I know which of those two options he'd prefer."

Rose felt the sting of tears at her friend's unwavering support but tried to hold them back. From the expression on Catherine's face, it was clear she hadn't been entirely successful.

"I'll speak to Louisa now and then inform Kerrick about our decision when he visits later. I'm sure we'll be able to call on Lord Brantford tomorrow since I know you won't want to wait."

Rose shook her head in amazement. "You're almost as tenacious as me. I'm not sure what I would have done without you."

Catherine gave her a hug, then pulled back with a fond smile. "After everything you did to make sure I got my happily-ever-after, it's the very least I can do. I can't help you clear your father's name, but I will help you to speak to the only man who possibly can."

24

BRANTFORD CLOSED THE LAST FILE and stopped just short of tossing it onto the alarmingly high stack of files that seemed to multiply on their own.

He hated this part of his occupation the most— reading reports. He already had mountains of accounts and letters related to his estate and properties that he needed to oversee. Despite having a more-than-capable steward, he wasn't foolish enough to trust the man completely. If his line of work had taught him anything, it was that any man could be corrupted with the right inducement.

He'd always had a good head for numbers, and it never took him long to look over the estate accounts. But when it came to matters concerning England's safety, it seemed the Home Office lived to bury him in minutiae. At least it had served to take his mind off the events at the Tower that morning.

The brisk knock at the door had him leaning back in his chair and stretching his tense shoulders. "Enter."

His butler opened the door and produced a small silver tray upon which had been placed a calling card. Brantford bit back a curse. It seemed his work was not yet done.

He released an annoyed breath when he saw Kerrick's name on the card. So much for putting Rose Hardwick from his mind.

"I'll see him here."

He was curious about the reason for the man's visit. When Kerrick entered and closed the door behind him, Brantford raised a brow. "This is a surprise."

Kerrick lowered himself into a chair Brantford kept to the side of his desk for the sole purpose of such meetings.

"I have news. I thought about including it in a report since I know how much you love those…" He eyed the pile on Brantford's desk and gave his head a small shake.

Brantford steepled his fingers and watched the other man with great care. "I thought you were out of it?"

Kerrick's mouth twisted downward. "I am, but one of my contacts finally got back to me with some information. Information you'd want to know since it might concern Rose."

Brantford couldn't hold back the annoyance that spiked whenever he heard Rose's name on the other man's lips, but he did everything in his power to hide it.

"By all means," he said, waiting for Kerrick to continue.

"It concerns Standish."

That caught Brantford's attention. Before Worthington's confession, Kerrick had told him Standish was somehow involved in this whole mess. He'd been seen arguing with Worthington, and soon after Rose's father had confessed to treason. But they'd been unable to find any proof that Standish was involved in selling secrets to the French.

"You can connect him to Worthington?"

Kerrick shook his head. "Unfortunately, no. Not yet. The man is more slippery than an eel. But my contact discovered some information about his background that his father had tried to conceal."

Brantford waited patiently for the other man to continue.

Kerrick's mouth turned down in disgust. "I don't know if you recall hearing about the death of his cousin years ago, when the old earl was still alive and Standish had yet to reach the age of majority."

Brantford nodded. It had been a messy business. The young woman had just come out, but sometime during that season she'd been found dead. Murdered, apparently, but her killer had never been identified. It seemed, however, that was no longer the case.

"Standish?"

Kerrick nodded. "He didn't just kill the girl. He raped her first, then strangled her."

Disgust and anger churned in Brantford's belly as he contemplated how black a man's soul had to be to commit such a crime. "So the man is a murderer and his father hid the scandal."

"Yes. He had Standish shipped off to the continent. Paid and threatened anyone who could testify as to his son's whereabouts at the time of the crime. Most of them disappeared, never to be heard from again."

"Until now."

"Yes, but don't expect Standish to pay for that crime. My contact tells me the person he spoke to is terrified of Standish and what he'll do to his family."

"Understandably so," Brantford said. "If the man had no qualms about killing his own cousin, he certainly wouldn't hesitate to hurt a stranger."

"Yes."

A thought that had been niggling at the edges of his mind finally took shape. "Didn't the old earl die under mysterious circumstances?"

Kerrick nodded. "We can only speculate, of course, but I wouldn't be surprised to learn that Standish had a hand in that as well."

Brantford ran through the ramifications of these new revelations, but they still didn't connect the man to treason. "He's quite wealthy now. He certainly doesn't need to sell secrets to the French."

"Not for money, no. But it would appear he might have a more personal reason for betraying the country."

"Don't make me ask," Brantford said when Kerrick didn't continue. He hated it when his agents tried to play guessing games with him. Then again, it was possible he was overreacting, not that he'd ever admit it. He still hadn't quite forgiven Kerrick for getting so close to Rose Hardwick.

"It appears that Standish's mother is French." At Brantford's raised brow, he continued. "Not the woman who raised him. The old earl's wife couldn't give him an heir, but his mistress fell pregnant and produced a son. A son that the earl passed off as being borne by his wife."

Brantford could see it all now. "By all accounts, the countess hated her son. Or, rather, hated the boy she'd raised as her son."

"Yes," Kerrick replied. "Can you imagine being raised by a woman who hated the very sight of you? Not that it excuses any of his crimes, but we can be certain the man has no notion of what family—or love—would look like."

They had that in common. Not the active hate part, of course, but Brantford had also been raised in a household devoid of familial warmth. That lack certainly didn't excuse Standish's actions.

"So you believe that Standish is selling secrets to the French... Why, exactly? As some kind of retribution against his pretend mother? Or against the man who'd taken him from his real mother and raised him in wealth and security?"

Kerrick burst from his chair and began to pace. "It's possible."

It was indeed, but they both knew they'd need more than that to connect him to Worthington's confession of treason.

"You've given me much to think about," Brantford

said, meaning it. The one thing they hadn't had was a reason for Standish to commit treason. Kerrick might just have uncovered his motive.

Kerrick stopped his restless movements and turned to face him. "I think Rose might be in danger from him."

His stomach actually dipped at those words. "Standish prefers his women to be fair-haired."

"Yes, and we both know he had his sights set on my betrothed. He gloated as much when he maneuvered me into the appearance of having compromised Rose. He was quite pleased with himself when I was forced to announce our engagement. With me out of the way, he thought he'd be able to get Catherine in his clutches. He wouldn't have, of course. Overlea is almost as fiercely protective of her as he is of his wife, and as her brother-in-law he has the means to keep Standish at bay. But Rose thwarted his plans when she told anyone who would listen that she'd broken our short-lived engagement."

Ice slithered through his veins. "And Standish isn't a man to be thwarted."

"No," Kerrick said. "Worthington confessed to protect his family. We can't prove that, but I feel it in my bones. But his confession might not be enough to protect Rose, not if Standish blames her for the fact that Catherine and I are now engaged. And if history is anything to go by, Standish *will* lash out when denied what he feels is his due."

Brantford said nothing, but he stood, shook Kerrick's

hand and thanked him for his information. The other man searched his expression, and Brantford must have betrayed more than he'd intended.

"I know you'll watch out for her," Kerrick said before exiting the room.

Brantford sank back into his chair, his emotions in tumult. He wanted to hit something, preferably Standish's face. He was sorely tempted to sweep the stack of reports from his desk, imagining the satisfaction to be gained from watching the paper scatter in every direction.

Instead, he clutched his hands into fists and closed his eyes, working to control his breathing and, with it, his temper. He made a silent vow to get to the bottom of this matter personally. He'd ensure Rose Hardwick remained safe.

BRANTFORD GLANCED DOWN at the hastily scrawled note his butler had handed him as he made his way to his study and allowed himself to scowl as he read it.

> *Planning to visit shortly with C, Lady O, and RH. The last wants to take you up on your offer to help.*
> *— Kerrick*

He dropped the note into a bin—wishing it wasn't too warm for a fire so he could burn the thing—and lowered himself into his desk chair. When he realized he was still scowling, he smoothed his brow.

Rose Hardwick was coming to his home. He didn't know why that idea unsettled him so much, but he wouldn't dwell on that now. Kerrick had kept Rose from visiting her father that morning. Maybe he'd be able to go one step further and convince her to join her mother in the country where she'd be safe.

Almost immediately he stood again. There was no point in pretending he was otherwise occupied when they arrived. He made his way to the drawing room where he summoned a footman and instructed him to bring refreshments as soon as his guests arrived. He wondered if Kerrick had known about this visit when they spoke yesterday. If so, he needn't have gone to the trouble of keeping it secret since Brantford wasn't about to turn Rose away. He doubted she knew anything about her father's dealings, but he wouldn't dismiss the opportunity to question her.

Perhaps this time she wouldn't be quite so angry with him. He had no reason to believe her waspishness toward him was personal. He imagined she was just lashing out and, given the amount of gossip and speculation swirling around her family at the moment, he couldn't blame her.

He wanted to pace, but he resisted the urge and lowered himself into an armchair. It took far more concentration than he would admit to keep his attention focused on the newspaper.

He only had to wait ten minutes before his butler

answered a knock at the door. He set aside the *Times* and rose to his feet only when the small group entered the room.

After greeting his guests, he waited for the women to take their seats on the settee before sitting again. Kerrick took the other armchair in the room.

"I wasn't expecting such charming company this morning." He couldn't stop his eyes from settling on Rose as he spoke. She'd gotten some rest since he last saw her, for the circles under her eyes were gone, but he could see signs of strain in the way her mouth tightened and in the stiff set of her shoulders. He tried to assess her mood, but she wouldn't look at him directly. It appeared he'd have to wait a bit longer to discover whether she was still taking her frustration out on him.

"I hope this isn't too much of an imposition," Lady Overlea said.

"Not at all," Brantford replied. Leaning back, he watched the group as the footman arrived, on schedule, with tea and a tray filled with an assortment of sweets.

"We all know why we're here," Kerrick said after Lady Overlea had poured tea for everyone. "Louisa and Catherine will stay here while the three of us discuss the reason for our visit privately."

Brantford narrowed his eyes, assessing everyone in the room. It did appear that Kerrick's betrothed and her sister were content to remain out of this discussion. But glancing at Rose, he realized he wouldn't get much information from her with the other man present. What had started off as a pretend courtship between them—

something that still irked him whenever he thought about it—had turned into Kerrick acting like a protective older brother toward Rose. He wouldn't get far if the other man insisted on speaking for her.

"I think it would be best if Miss Hardwick and I spoke alone."

Lady Overlea was surprised at his announcement. Catherine looked pleased, and he couldn't help but wonder why. Kerrick, however, was about to protest when Rose herself finally spoke.

"I think Lord Brantford is correct. I appreciate everything you're all doing for me, taking me in and making sure I'm not harassed when I visit Papa, but you can't continue to shield me."

"Just so," Brantford said, standing quickly before anyone could attempt to change her mind. "If you'll follow me."

Kerrick stood as well, his arms crossed. "Tread carefully," he said as Rose followed him from the room.

Brantford ignored him. He'd set these events in motion when he'd asked Kerrick to investigate Rose's father. He could hardly blame the other man for feeling some responsibility for the repercussions.

Brantford moved past his study—the last thing he needed was memories of Rose invading his inner sanctum while he was trying to work—and headed for the library. He allowed her to precede him into the room.

"We shouldn't be disturbed here even with the door open."

She gave a little shake of her head. "I have no doubt that my virtue is safe with you."

It shouldn't have struck him as an odd thing for her to say. She was, after all, alone with him, far enough away from her friends that he could do almost anything to her. What's more, almost as soon as that thought occurred to him, he realized he was also annoyed. He might be known for his carefully cultivated reserve, but he was hardly a monk. And it bothered him more than he wanted to admit that Rose Hardwick would think she was safe alone with him.

In actuality, she wasn't.

"Please, have a seat," he said, waiting for her to choose one of the chairs in front of the window before sitting opposite her. "First, I should ask why you are here."

"I think that's obvious," she said, her posture stiff as her eyes met his before gliding away again.

"I don't suppose you have any evidence to share with me that supports your father's claim that he has committed treason."

He'd wanted to shake her, elicit some kind of emotion from her other than resignation.

She stood, fingers gripping her reticule tightly while she glared at him. "This was a mistake. You can't help me."

He rose swiftly, holding her gaze while he bade her to sit down again. When she did so after several seconds, he continued. "You would be surprised what I can do.

But first I need you to talk to me. This won't work if we have to talk through Kerrick."

The air seemed to go out of her lungs, and she slumped down slightly. He waited.

"My father didn't commit treason." He was about to interject, but she spoke over him. "I know, he confessed. But he's not guilty. He *can't* be guilty."

"All right."

"All right? That's all you have to say?"

"You still haven't told me what you want from me."

Rose let out a small huff of annoyance. "You're insufferable, as I'm sure you are aware."

He allowed himself a small smile at that, happier than he'd ever admit to seeing a small hint of Rose's former spirit. "I may have heard that once or twice in my lifetime."

She stared at him for several seconds, and he found himself wishing he could read minds. There was something in her expression when she looked at him that unsettled him. But almost as quickly as he'd seen it, the emotion was gone.

"I need your assistance in proving his innocence. I've been told that if anyone can help me, it would be you."

He allowed her statement to sit there, heavy in the air, for several moments before replying. "What exactly have you been told?"

"Very little, actually." It was evident to him that fact annoyed her. "Last week, when I saw you at Kerrick's home, you wished me luck in exonerating my father.

Well, you were correct. Papa won't speak to me about what happened, and I don't know what to do."

"He's trying to protect you." He hated the bitter laugh that comment elicited.

"If he wanted to protect me, he wouldn't have confessed to a crime he didn't commit. What did he think would happen? That Mama and I would go on as we had been? And what about him? Mama is sick with worry about him."

"I believe," he said, weighing each word, "it was enough for him that the two of you remained alive."

CHAPTER 4

SHE COULDN'T HOLD BACK HER GASP. "What are you saying?"

"I'm saying that you should have followed your mother's example and left London. You aren't safe here."

Rose could only stare at him, unsure how she should take his ridiculous remark. She wanted to believe Brantford was exaggerating. That he was trying to shock her for some reason. But the more she thought about it, the more his assertion made sense.

The only motive her father would have for confessing to treason would be if he feared for their safety. But surely that belief had no basis in reality.

"Papa was mistaken," she said. "There is no reason for anyone to harm Mama and me."

"There are more things in heaven and earth—"

"Yes, yes. 'Than are dreamt of in your philosophy.' I know Shakespeare as well. You needn't act so superior."

He raised a brow at that, and she imagined he was annoyed at her outburst. She hated how superior and remote he acted. And, heaven help her, she hated that she found him all the more attractive because of it. Oh, to be the woman who would break through all that cool reserve. But that would never be her. Not anymore. Brantford would never court the daughter of a traitor.

"The fact remains that you would be safer in the country with your mother."

She stood, needing to move to work through her annoyance at his remark. He stood as well, the movement almost casual, and watched her. She sighed and sank back down into her seat, watching him follow suit. In that moment, she hated the convention that dictated a gentleman should stand when a lady did.

"Mama is grieving for my father. She is in pain, but she is also hiding from society. I won't hide. I need to be here to support him."

"You're placing yourself in unnecessary jeopardy. At the very least, you need to promise me that you'll refrain from visiting your father again."

She clenched her hands together at that remark but managed not to lash out at him. "I can't make that promise."

She stilled, shocked, when Brantford leaned forward in his chair, all his cool reserve seeming to fade in that instant, replaced by a heat in his pale blue eyes that she'd never expected to see.

"I'm afraid I must insist."

"I don't take orders from you," she managed to

reply. She hated the thrill of awareness that sparked through her at his shift in demeanor. Something changed in his face, and she wondered if he could sense her emotions.

"You believe your father is innocent, fine. I'll concede there is a slight possibility that is true. But he isn't foolish enough to admit to a crime that would see him hanged and his family's reputation ruined if the danger wasn't real."

She wanted to insist that he was wrong, but he held up a hand to silence her. "Allow me to continue, please. Has it occurred to you that the person your father might be trying to protect you from—and as you say, you don't think it was your father who actually committed treason —might take your visits to your father as a threat to his safety? He'll wonder if your father has told you anything that might point the finger to the real culprit. That, my dear, makes you a danger to him. But if you ceased your visits, he would have no reason to worry about your involvement."

Rose mulled over Brantford's statements and had to admit he had a valid point. After all, wasn't that exactly what she'd been hoping to accomplish? To convince her father to give her information that might exonerate him? Information that might point to the real perpetrator of the crime?

"Papa wasn't happy that I visited him. I thought it was because he was ashamed."

"He should be ashamed," Brantford said, and her hackles rose at his calm, detached tone. "He's either a traitor or he's somehow entangled with one. Neither of those alternatives paints him in a good light."

She wanted to deny it, to come up with a scathing comment that would put Brantford firmly in his place, but she couldn't. Whatever the real story, her father had gotten himself involved in something unsavory. Something that apparently put her life in jeopardy.

She looked down at her hands, overwhelmed by the enormity of the task she'd undertaken but unwilling to admit defeat quite yet. "I don't know what to do."

When he reached across the small distance that separated their chairs and placed one hand over hers, she stilled in shock. She was wearing gloves, but he wasn't, and to her unexpected delight, his hand was warm. The heat seemed to seep through the thin cotton covering her hands, bringing her a measure of comfort. No doubt that was all he'd intended with the action.

"I'll help you," he said. "I don't know how to convince your father to give me the information I know he's hiding, but I'll find a way. But you have to promise me you'll stay away from the Tower."

She opened her mouth to reply, but he squeezed her hand then, silencing her. "I need you to do this for me. I can't be effective if I'm worrying about you."

She lifted her eyes to his, shocked at the sincerity she saw reflected in his gaze. Lord Brantford—the Unaffected Earl—was worried for her.

She nodded, unable to speak.

He searched her face and must have seen she wasn't

lying. With a slight nod, he removed his hand and straightened in his chair.

"Fine. Now, tell me what you know about events leading up to that evening."

She told him everything she could recall but was afraid it wasn't much help. "Papa tried to shelter me. I know things were difficult for a little while. Mama told me she didn't think I'd have a season. But then everything changed."

"Did you notice any changes in your father's behavior?"

She knew why he was asking the question, but she had to hold back her annoyance.

"Honestly? No. He was worried before about our financial situation, I think." At the questioning lift of his brow, she explained. "My father tried to shelter me, but that doesn't mean I didn't know what was happening. Not the details, of course. But when Mama told me that we'd be going to London after all, I thought that meant our financial constraints had eased. But Papa was just as tense when we arrived in town."

"Did your father have any private meetings at the house?"

Rose had to look away at the question. "I can provide you with a list of names of those who've spoken with him. I don't know if it would be a complete list, but there were more than a few of whom I was aware."

She was embarrassed, suddenly, to admit that many, if not all, of those meetings were with men who wanted to court her.

"Yes, I imagine there were."

The slight tightening of his jaw left her wondering what he was thinking. It would be pointless to ask, however. He'd only tell her what he wanted her to know.

"What do we do now?"

"Now we'll return to the drawing room, and you'll have some tea. Then tomorrow I'll send someone to escort you to your town house. I've already had someone search your father's study—"

"What?" Rose frowned in puzzlement.

Brantford had his mask firmly in place, and she couldn't tell what he was thinking when he replied. "As you've no doubt already suspected, I've been looking into this matter for some time, searching for evidence as to who else might be involved."

"For how long?"

"Some time. Now, may I continue?"

She nodded, her mind whirling with the implications of his admission. Brantford had been investigating her father, possibly even before her father had confessed to treason. Had he known what was happening?

"I will send someone I trust implicitly to meet you at Overlea's town house and escort you to your home. In the event your movements are being watched, she'll make sure you're safe. I'll meet you there."

"But if your neighbors see you pay a call on me, when I'm home alone, they'll think the worst." Heat flooded her cheeks as she realized how absurd her statement was. "Never mind. I'm sure everyone already thinks the worst. I'll never marry well now. The best I can do is to accept an offer to become someone's mistress. No doubt men are just lining up for the opportunity to offer me carte blanche once I leave the protection of Catherine's family."

She stood abruptly and turned away from him. His hand on her shoulder, no doubt meant to comfort her, only served to make her feel even more ashamed.

"No one will see me," he assured her.

"Perhaps not, but that doesn't change my situation."

He said nothing to that, and she forced back her embarrassment. Brantford was a man of the world. He probably had his own mistress, though her mind shied away from trying to imagine what she would look like.

"I apologize for my outburst," she said, turning back to face him.

She told herself she hadn't seen concern on his face before he nodded. He offered her his arm and escorted her back to the drawing room.

She tried not to worry about tomorrow. She could only hope that whatever they found would exonerate her father.

CHAPTER 5

ROSE WASN'T SURE WHOM SHE'D BEEN EXPECTING, but it wasn't the matronly woman currently waiting for her in the front hall of Catherine's home.

"Please come in," she said, wondering why the butler hadn't shown her into the drawing room.

"There's no need," the stranger said. "We can speak in the carriage on the way."

Rose turned to Catherine, who'd joined her downstairs when the butler announced that Rose had a visitor. "It appears I'm leaving right away with…"

"Oh, it's Mrs. Ellen Blackwell."

"Very well, Mrs. Blackwell. It's very nice to meet you."

"And you as well," the older woman said, a hint of what might have been curiosity on her face. Rose couldn't imagine what else would be behind the speculative gleam in her eye.

"Do you need me to come with you?" Catherine asked.

"Oh no," Mrs. Blackwell said. "We'll be fine, just the two of us."

Catherine looked to Rose for confirmation. "Are you sure?"

Before she could reply, Mrs. Blackwell said, "Quite."

Rose shrugged. "Apparently I'm sure."

Her friend's brows drew together, but she said nothing further. Rose told her she'd be back before too long, although she really had no idea how long today's activity would take, and turned to follow the other woman from the house. The carriage that was waiting outside was a utilitarian vehicle, its lines plain, the color dark. Unlikely to draw attention.

As soon as the vehicle drew away from the house, Rose could no longer hold back her questions. "You weren't what I was expecting, Mrs. Blackwell. From the fuss Lord Brantford made about my safety, I thought he'd send a team of burly men to guard my person."

Mrs. Blackwell laughed. "Oh, I like you. I can see that Brantford might very well have met his match. And you needn't be so formal. You can call me Ellen."

"All right, Ellen," she said, deciding not to ask the woman what she'd meant lest she betray her unseemly interest in Brantford.

"Go ahead and ask," Ellen said. "I can see you're dying to know everything about me and how I'm connected to Lord B."

Rose felt her eyes widen, wondering if her

companion actually called Brantford that to his face. She couldn't imagine it but would love to see it. "Lord B?"

Ellen smiled. "Well, in our line of work, it doesn't do to refer to each other by our names. Being cryptic is a habit I find myself falling into without even being aware I'm doing it."

Rose tilted her head to the side, wondering if she could finally get the answers she wanted. "And your line of work would be…?"

Ellen shook her head. "If you don't already know, I'm not going to be the one to tell you. Brantford would have my hide."

Rose crossed her arms and glared at the woman, but it was mainly for show. If Catherine wouldn't tell her what she knew, she could hardly expect this stranger to reveal everything.

"Fine. Lord Brantford can keep his secrets. I'm sure he has many, and they're of no concern to me. All I require from him is his assistance in proving my father's innocence."

Ellen didn't reply, and Rose could feel the older woman's eyes examining her as the silence stretched between them. It took a great deal of effort not to squirm under that gaze.

"Brantford is quite handsome, wouldn't you say?"

"I… What?" Rose saw a gleam enter the other woman's eyes at her stumble and hated the fact that she'd betrayed herself so thoroughly. "I suppose, if you like men who are cold and distant."

"I daresay many women do. The lure of being the one to break through his icy facade has been a temptation to many. I should warn you that, to a one, they've all failed."

Rose looked away, pretending to take in the scenery outside the carriage window. "I don't see why I should care about any of that."

"I'm not here to lecture you, despite the appearance to the contrary. I just wanted to warn you that Brantford comes by his moniker honestly. If there's a heart buried somewhere beneath his surface, he keeps it well hidden."

Rose's thoughts went back to the previous morning, when Brantford's mask had slipped in her presence, and suddenly began to doubt what she'd imagined had taken place between them. In all probability, she'd seen only what she'd wanted to see. Brantford's concern for her well-being was likely no different than what he'd show anyone who found themselves in the same position.

She sighed and met the other woman's gaze. "I understand. And I thank you for the warning."

"You think I'm harsh."

"No, you're just being honest." She hesitated a moment before continuing, but it appeared Ellen already knew about her tendre for Brantford. Heaven knew how. Perhaps this was a warning she gave all women who came near him. The thought that she was just one of many foolish women who'd set their sights on him was more than a little depressing.

"You appear to know him well."

"Quite well. And no, not in that way. Brantford is

hardly likely to align himself with a woman who resembles his mother more than anything else."

There was something about the way Ellen Blackwell casually dismissed the statement that caught Rose's attention. She examined the other woman closely and realized she'd missed the telltale signs that the woman was not all that she seemed.

"You say that as though it were completely out of the question. I can see now that you're not as old as you're trying to appear. And the gray in your fair hair?" She leaned forward and saw the hint of light powder dotting the woman's shoulders. "Powder, if I'm not mistaken."

Ellen's mouth fell open and she collapsed back on the bench. She stared at Rose for several seconds before saying, "I underestimated you."

Rose couldn't hold back her laugh, relieved that she'd guessed correctly. "The lines around your eyes and mouth?"

"Stage makeup," Ellen said.

Rose nodded. "It's very convincing. Most people wouldn't notice, but in the country, with very little to do, my friends and I have taken to putting on performances for one another. Complete, of course, with some rather amusing attempts at disguising ourselves for our roles."

Ellen examined her for several seconds before speaking. "Forget what I said."

"Of course," Rose said. "I won't tell a soul. It makes sense that you would need to disguise yourself before being seen in my company."

Ellen gave her a sympathetic smile. "No, not that. And for the record, I would have no problem being seen in your company whatever my guise. What I meant to say was that I wanted you to ignore what I said about Brantford."

Now Rose was completely confused. "You haven't told me anything. All I have is wild speculation."

"No," Ellen said with a small shake of her head. "Forget what I said about all those other women. You might be just what Brantford needs."

It was June and uncommonly warm that day, but Rose feared that the heat that engulfed her in that moment would be accompanied by a very revealing blush.

"Everything you said still applies."

"Yes, unfortunately, it does." Ellen's mouth turned downward.

"So, you and he never…"

"He's my brother."

That was the last thing Rose expected to hear, but it brought her a measure of relief. Ellen was a very striking woman in her current guise. Without the makeup that made her appear as though she were past her prime, Rose expected she would be quite beautiful.

"I don't recall seeing you at any of the events this season, and I've been to more than my fair share of them."

"I don't socialize very often," Ellen said.

Rose wanted to ask more, suddenly fascinated by the woman in front of her. The way her expression had closed off, however, told her that any further questions on the subject wouldn't be welcome.

"Lord Brantford hasn't shown even the slightest hint that he returns my ill-conceived infatuation with him." She waved a hand at the way Ellen raised one slim brow. "There's no point in pretending. You've already said as much."

"That's true, but most young ladies would continue to pretend indifference."

"I've always found honesty to be much better. Oh, I'll admit that I've flirted with the best of them and encouraged other men in their own infatuations. It's all a game, you see, and helps to pass the time during all those events. But I've always hated the way women feel as though they are in competition with one another. Such a waste."

"Indeed," Ellen said, her smile widening.

Rose could almost see the wheels turning in the other woman's mind but decided there was no point in saying anything more on the subject. Despite what Ellen said, nothing had changed.

She'd just have to keep reminding herself of that fact.

EMOTION ASSAILED HER when she walked into her family's town house. Little more than a week had passed since their entire world had been turned upside down, but the house seemed so foreign now. Quiet. Sad, as though it too were in mourning for the abrupt change in their circumstances.

When she unlocked the front door, she expected their butler or a footman to greet her but instead was met only with silence. She realized then that Brantford must have arranged to give the staff the day off. It would hardly do for them to be seen meeting in private, even with a chaperone.

She turned to Ellen, who'd closed the door behind her. "When is Lord Brantford expected?"

"I'm already here."

Awareness of his presence caused Rose's skin to prickle, but she managed to maintain her reserve when she turned to face him. He was striding down the hall.

"Have you had the opportunity to ransack all the rooms in the house yet?" She couldn't hold back her irritation even though she knew it was senseless. After all, they were there to search for information her father might have concealed.

"Not quite," he said, his tone infuriatingly even. "I've only just arrived. We've already discreetly searched the house, but it was difficult to be thorough with the staff present. The powers that be thought it a waste of time, but I managed to convince them otherwise. You should know that it took no small effort to coax your butler to leave today, and I had to personally assure him that we wouldn't turn everything upside down. Despite what's happened, he's very loyal to your family."

Rose sighed, feeling wistful as she imagined the taciturn older man who'd always had a soft spot for her. She wondered how much longer it would be before he and the rest of the staff were lured away to other positions.

"Mrs. Blackwell, thank you for joining us today."

Ellen tilted her head and smiled up at her brother. "She knows who I am."

He shook his head. "Of course she does. I would have thought that of all people, you would be able to resist her charms."

Ellen replied, but Rose didn't hear what she'd said. Had Brantford just admitted that he found her alluring?

She chastised herself for the hope that sparked in her heart. He was probably referring to the gaggle of men who used to seek her out. He could acknowledge that others were drawn to her but not feel any hint of attraction himself.

She shook her head to clear it of her confusing muddle of thoughts.

"You don't agree?" Ellen asked.

"I'm sorry," Rose said. "I was thinking about something else. I didn't hear what you suggested."

The other woman gave her a sympathetic smile. "Of course. I imagine it must be difficult for you to be here. We were saying that since Brantford has started searching your father's study, he should finish there and then move on to the library. We can search the bedrooms upstairs."

Rose frowned. "Papa kept his important papers in his study. Do we really need to look through the bedrooms?"

"It's possible he would have hidden information

where no one would think to look." Brantford's voice was uncharacteristically soft when he spoke, missing his normal detachment.

Rose told herself she was imagining things as she nodded and followed Ellen upstairs.

Rose directed Brantford's sister to her mother's room and proceeded to her father's bedroom. She told herself that what they were doing was necessary. They had to find something—anything—that would prove her father had confessed to his crime under coercion from an outside source. But it still felt wrong to be going through his things. She imagined there wouldn't be much for Ellen to search since her mother had arranged to have her personal belongings sent to her aunt's house in Essex.

Rose made quick work of opening drawers, examining the wardrobe, and even looking under the mattress. It was a habit to hide her own diary in the last place. Fortunately, she didn't have to worry about Ellen or, heaven forbid, Brantford stumbling across it as her diary was now safely residing under the mattress in her guest bedroom at Overlea's town house.

"We should search your room," Ellen said from the doorway.

Rose frowned. "I already know what's in my room, and there's nothing of interest there."

"Humor me," Ellen said. "You'd be surprised what people hide in their children's rooms, thinking no one would look there. I'll finish in here."

Rose looked around the room and shrugged before turning to leave.

"Look under the carpets," Ellen called out as she bent down to do the same in her father's bedroom.

That never would have occurred to her, but then again, she'd only ever had cause to hide her journal. She supposed it would be easier to hide a letter under the carpet. But wouldn't it crinkle if one stepped on it?

She froze as a thought occurred to her.

If a floorboard had been removed and something hidden beneath that, it might make a creaking sound. Something like the groan that was emitted when one stepped too close to the window in the library.

Moving past her bedroom, she raced downstairs toward that room, her heart pounding. She hesitated when she saw Brantford was already there, easing a group of books back into place.

"It's going to take forever to examine each one of these books to see if there are any documents hidden within their pages or if any of them are hollow." He turned to face her. "I'll have someone come in later to do that."

Rose gave him an absent nod and moved to the north-facing window. The curtains were closed, as always, despite the fact she always made a point to open them whenever she walked into the room. She'd always assumed the servants closed them, but perhaps there was a different reason. Her father might have instructed they be kept closed so as not to chance anyone looking inside from the neighbor's window and seeing what he was doing.

She stepped on the floorboard just to the left of the window and, as if on cue, it emitted a groaning sound. She noticed that Brantford was watching her and did her best to ignore him as she stepped back. Taking a deep breath, she crouched down and turned up the edge of the carpet.

The floorboards looked normal. She sighed, a mixture of disappointment and relief filling her. She was about to let the carpet fall back into place when Brantford crouched down next to her.

"Not yet."

Her heart was racing as he prodded around the floorboards, but it wasn't entirely from their task. He was so close she could feel the warmth emanating from him. She wondered how someone with a reputation for being so cold and remote could generate so much heat.

She kept her eyes down, somehow resisting the temptation to examine his face, and watched his hands instead.

He quickly zeroed in on one board and reached into an inner coat pocket. She gasped when he flicked a button on the onyx cylinder he produced and a blade popped out.

His eyes went to hers, an indescribable emotion hidden in their depths, before he bent, again, to the task at hand. Using the knife to edge underneath the floorboard, he soon had it removed completely.

Rose's heart almost stopped when she saw the

slender box concealed underneath the board. She released the carpet, only noticing then that Brantford was holding it down with one knee, and rose swiftly.

He followed, the box in one hand, his other hand reaching back into his coat. No doubt he was concealing the blade again.

She took several steps back, her eyes glued to the box. A box that might hold proof of her father's innocence. Or it could contain the opposite. "I don't want to know what's in there. Yet at the same time, I do."

He placed it on a table before turning back to face her. "There's a lock. I can open it later, after we've finished searching the house."

She licked her bottom lip, noticing the way his eyes zeroed in on the movement. In another time, another place, she could have been accused of using that small motion as an attempt to draw the attention of the man standing before her, but she could honestly say that hadn't been her intention. She hadn't even been aware she was doing it until she noticed the way his gaze had flickered down to her mouth.

A riot of nerves assailed her, and she took a step back. "Ellen is probably waiting for me in my room. I raced down here without telling her of my suspicions."

A corner of his mouth lifted, and she could only stare at him for several seconds. She didn't think it possible that she could find him more handsome than she already did. She was wrong.

"Are you nervous around me?"

Good heavens, was Brantford flirting with her? Or

was she reading something more into their exchange simply because he'd smiled at her?

"I…" She took a deep breath, determined not to let him win this little game. For in that moment, and with striking clarity, she knew that was what this was to him. A game. Well, she'd played this particular sport before and had always won.

Taking a step closer to him, she tilted her head and smiled. "Not at all, my lord."

His face was once again an impassive mask, and she could tell he didn't want her to know what he was thinking.

She took another step closer. "I think we both know that I'm safe with you."

He moved so quickly she had no time to react. He stood barely a breath away, and her heart began to race again. "Is that what you think? If you truly knew what I wanted to do to you, you'd run screaming."

There was the slightest of hitches in his voice, which was all the confirmation she needed that he wasn't unaffected by her.

A thrill of delight went through her. "I'm not running," she said, surprised at the hint of breathlessness in her voice.

His eyes roamed over her face, and she willed him to lean forward and kiss her. She yearned for it, and she could tell that he was tempted. Instead, he stepped back.

"You'd be wise to reconsider."

His tone was even again and she couldn't hold back her sigh of disappointment. He might be drawn to her, but it was clear he would never give in to that temptation.

Ellen's earlier warning rang loudly in her mind, and she chided herself for being foolish enough to think anything could ever happen between them. "Of course," she said, turning without another word and making her way upstairs.

BRANTFORD WATCHED HER GO, unwilling to concede that Rose Hardwick might very well have succeeded where no one else ever had. She'd stirred his emotions. He didn't just want her physically… he longed to possess that generous, surprisingly clever mind of hers.

He'd been struck by her rare beauty when he'd first started investigating Worthington. He'd watched her flirt with nearly every unwed man in the *ton*, and she'd had them all eating out of her hand. He was no callow youth to be taken in by a pretty face, however.

But then she'd shown her unswerving loyalty to her father and to her new friend, Catherine Evans. In so doing, she'd proven herself generous to a fault. Kerrick had been cornered into offering to marry Rose despite caring deeply for Catherine. Any other woman would have clung to the protection his name could provide when her family's reputation fell apart. Instead, Rose had broken the betrothal, and she'd done so in a public manner that ensured Kerrick wouldn't have to sacrifice his feelings for her new friend.

And despite what he'd said to his sister, he knew Ellen never would have told her of their relationship, not without any prodding. No, Rose must have seen through his sister's disguise, something which almost never happened. People generally saw what they expected to see, after all.

He would never admit it to Rose, of course, but she intrigued him more than he wanted to admit.

CHAPTER 6

*T*HIS TIME BRANTFORD ACCOMPANIED ROSE when she visited her father at the Tower. Between Kerrick's warning about Standish and the lack of any new information, he had no choice but to use Worthington's desire to protect his daughter against him.

Despite his hope to the contrary, the hidden box they'd uncovered revealed nothing that they didn't already know. It held copies of Worthington's financial records, which showed that large sums of money had been deposited into his bank account on two occasions over the past few months.

When Rose asked about the contents of the box after he examined it, he merely told her it held nothing they could use to free her father. He could tell that she'd wanted to question him further but instead had turned away from him, her shoulders slumped and her head lowered. He'd wanted to comfort her, had somehow restrained himself from reaching out for her.

Their visit today wasn't wise, but they were at an impasse. Bringing Rose further into it put her life at increased danger, but he knew she was willing to do whatever was necessary to help her father. If he didn't include her in his investigation, she'd go off on her own, and then he wouldn't be able to keep her safe.

His worry for Rose's safety wasn't a new sensation for him. Every time he asked for Ellen's assistance, he had cause to worry that he was putting her in danger. But he preferred to know where she was and what she was doing than be distracted wondering who she was working with now and what dangers she was facing.

His sister was more than capable of taking care of herself, he'd seen to her training himself, but there was only so much she could do against a much larger assailant. Or, heaven forbid, against a group of them, a situation he'd found her in the one time he'd allowed her to work with another agent. Under his watch, he could ensure she never found herself in such dire straits again.

If Standish was involved, and his instincts told him that he was, Brantford needed to know if he was acting alone. Time was also a pressing concern. If Worthington didn't give them something to go on, the real culprit would continue to operate unhindered. Brantford had been able to delay Worthington's execution, but that could change if the older man refused to cooperate with his investigation.

For Rose's sake, he found himself hoping to discover

evidence that her father had been coerced in some way. Then he could send Rose Hardwick on her way and go about the task of putting her out of his mind. He didn't know what had possessed him to reveal he found her desirable the day before, but he was determined to ensure it never happened again.

He'd pressed his sister into service again and was currently waiting for them in a carriage outside the Overlea town house. Normally, he would have met them at the Tower, but he needed to speak to Rose before they saw her father. He paid no attention to the relief he felt knowing that he wouldn't be alone with her.

When a footman opened the carriage door, the slight widening of Rose's eyes told him she was surprised to see him. He ignored the slight amusement on his sister's face when their eyes met.

"I apologize for not meeting you outside," he said by way of greeting when the two women were safely inside the carriage.

Rose waved her hand in dismissal. "I understand. Society's rules must go by the wayside when one is engaged in the business of spy work."

He had to fight against the urge to look at his sister, curious as to whether she'd let that information slip as well. With any luck, Rose was just guessing and hoping to catch him out. That she'd guessed correctly was beside the point.

The way she huffed in annoyance and crossed her arms just below her breasts told him he'd been correct. He couldn't help but notice the way her breasts looked, framed by her bodice and her bare arms, but he refused to break eye contact with her. He would not to be so easily distracted.

"We have matters to discuss before we see your father."

She inclined her head, and he wondered, briefly, if she was trying to copy his own mannerisms or if she was annoyed with him.

"I've spoken to your father, but he refuses to discuss his reason for confessing to treason. He has insisted that he acted alone but couldn't—or wouldn't—tell me who he sold the secrets to."

"That's because he doesn't know. Someone else sold those secrets."

"Perhaps. Perhaps not. But we're going to need to rattle him to get him to reveal anything, and that is why I requested your presence today."

"You said it wasn't safe for me to visit my father. Has that changed?"

He ignored the stab of guilt. "No, it hasn't. But it's recently come to my attention that you are already at risk. We must do all that we can to put an end to this matter."

He noticed the way Ellen reached out to take Rose's hand and the way Rose smiled at his sister. He put aside his annoyance at not being able to offer her similar comfort.

"I've made arrangements for Ellen to stay with you, and Kerrick has already spoken to Overlea about adding a few of my men to the household staff to pose as footmen."

Rose slumped back against the seat and closed her eyes, sighing loudly. "This is a nightmare. The last thing I want to do is place Catherine or her family at risk, not when they've been so kind and welcoming to me." She took a deep breath before meeting his eyes again. "I should return to my family's town house. Ellen can stay with me there, and the men can be added to our household staff."

He shook his head. "That won't work. You'll be vulnerable there, alone."

"I won't—"

"Miss Evans is also in danger. With the two of you under the same roof, it is easier to keep both of you safe. Overlea is a good man. He's already protective of his wife and sister-in-law. Other than you staying with me—which we all know is out of the question—his home is the safest place for you."

To his surprise, Rose brushed off his concerns for her safety and zeroed in on the implied threat to her friend. "Catherine is in danger? It's because of me, is it not?"

He hadn't particularly wanted to share this information with her, but she'd hear it soon enough. He needed to dangle this piece of bait in front of her father to get him to speak.

"It's because of Lord Standish."

Rose shuddered. "That man is horrible. There's something cold about him. Unnatural. And the way he kept circling around Catherine." She shuddered again. "I tried to distract her whenever he was present, but I wasn't able to keep him from dancing with her."

Why was he surprised that Rose had picked up on the unsavory aspects of the other man's character? She might not know the details about Standish's past, but it was clear she had excellent instincts.

"What do you know about him?"

"Nothing beyond the feeling that he's someone whom I should stay away from. He's never shown any interest in me though. Only Catherine."

"Do you know whether your father had occasion to meet with him privately?"

He forced himself not to dwell on the way her nose scrunched as she concentrated. He certainly didn't think it was adorable.

"Not that I remember. Wait…"

Her eyes widened as something occurred to her. "Lord Standish. He was there, at the ball, when Lord Kerrick and I were found alone together. He entered the room just behind my parents. Was he responsible for everything that evening? Lord Kerrick said he received a note that he thought was from Catherine. I thought mine was from… someone else."

The way her eyes slithered away, a hint of color touching her cheeks, had him curious about whom it was she'd been hoping to see. If she favored one of the men who followed her around everywhere, surely he would have noticed. Not because he'd been watching her, of course. His interest had only been on investigating her father.

He met Ellen's eyes then, and his sister arched one delicate brow as she glanced down at his hands. Only then did he realize he was clenching his fists. He forced his hands to relax and looked at Rose again.

"Standish wanted Kerrick out of the way so he could pursue Catherine himself. When you broke your engagement, you thwarted his plans."

Rose stared at him, her mouth open in horror. "I never thought to wonder about it. Things happened so quickly after that, and then Papa confessed to treason. Surely Lord Standish will just move on to someone else. Though I don't envy the poor girl who will receive his attentions."

"We don't believe he is one to give up so easily." At Rose's frown, he continued, "Catherine should be safe enough. Between Overlea and Kerrick, they have her locked up tight. You should be safe there, as well, from any action Standish should wish to take in revenge."

Rose shook her head. "This makes no sense. What would he do to me? Unless…" He saw the moment she realized the truth. "You think Standish is involved in this crime. That it is he, not my father, who committed treason and he somehow coerced my father to confess."

"It remains to be seen whether or not your father was a willing participant." Rose frowned at that, but he ignored her displeasure and continued. "I believe your father confessed because he was worried that Standish was a real threat to you and your mother."

Rose sank back against the seat again. "This is a nightmare. What are we going to do? Should we confront Lord Standish?"

A flash of annoyance—and if he were being completely honest with himself, more than a hint of fear —swept through him at the notion. He leaned forward, intent on imparting the seriousness of his next words. "Under no circumstances are you to go anywhere near Lord Standish."

She narrowed her eyes. "But if he is the person responsible—"

"I don't think your father would thank you if you proved his innocence only to end up in the grave."

His words had shocked her. Good. He'd meant them to shake an ounce of rational thought into her head. If nothing else, Rose had to stay as far away from Standish as possible.

"You honestly think that's true?"

"Yes."

"Does…" She swallowed visibly before continu- ing. "Does Kerrick know about Lord Standish? He must. You're friends, and if you know what happened between the two of us, and if you know that Lord Standish—" Her voice hitched as she said his name. "If you know that he has designs on Catherine…"

When she faltered, Ellen spoke. "What is it you want to know?"

"Were you already investigating my father? Did you suspect him of wrongdoing before he confessed? And was Lord Kerrick involved in that investigation? Catherine said something that has me wondering."

His eyes narrowed only a fraction, but it was enough for her to notice.

"You needn't scowl at me like that. She didn't actually tell me anything. Only that you were well connected. But I realize now that the only way she would know something like that is if her betrothed is also involved in whatever it is that you do."

What should he say? He wanted to tell her nothing, but in that moment he could understand how Kerrick had let Catherine discover far more than she ever should have. He'd vowed he would never be that weak, but here he was, a scant few weeks later, finding himself on the precipice of doing the very same thing.

"None of this is relevant to the task at hand."

"It's relevant to me." Her eyes flashed with fire, her chest heaved, as she continued. "Kerrick was pursuing me despite the fact that he was in love with another woman. Why would he do that unless he was ordered to? Ordered by you, no doubt."

He said nothing.

She made a small sound of distress that had him itching to comfort her. "Does Catherine know?" She shook her head, her curls bouncing with the movement. "Of course she knows. I spent weeks trying to get her to be more assertive toward Lord Kerrick, telling her that he cared for her and not me, and yet she continued to do nothing. She allowed him to court me even though she loved him and she knew I cared for another."

With all her distress, the one thing that caught his attention was her very last statement. Rose loved someone else. It took every ounce of willpower he possessed not to ask who.

"Is her friendship real? Or was she involved in all this as well?"

"I can assure you that any friendship on her part was offered without any instruction from Kerrick or me."

She looked away from him, unable or unwilling to respond. He attempted to give her a small measure of comfort when he said, "Miss Evans is not good with deceit. What you see is what you get with her. If she tells you that she is your friend, you can rest assured she's being genuine."

"I can't talk about this right now," Rose said after almost a full minute of silence. "Was there something more you wanted to tell me about Lord Standish before we speak to my father?"

Brantford found it more difficult than he'd ever admit to focus on the task at hand—their upcoming meeting with her father. He gave her a short nod even though she was still looking away and didn't see it.

"You've already told me that you'd do what was necessary to help your father, correct?"

"Yes," she said, her tone devoid of all emotion. She met his eyes briefly, then looked away again.

"We need to discover what your father is hiding. He's already sacrificed everything to protect you and your mother. To make him tell us the truth, we're going to need him to believe that your life is in immediate jeopardy from Lord Standish."

Rose crossed her arms again, and this time Brantford couldn't stop his eyes from dropping briefly to her breasts.

"I won't lie to my father," she said, glaring at him.

Good. He preferred Rose with her fire intact, not the lost creature she'd been only moments before. He avoided looking at his sister, knowing she would have seen the small lapse in his normal reserve.

"You won't need to. I'll do any fabricating that may be necessary. I only ask that you don't contradict me. Not if you want your father to tell me what he knows." She didn't reply, and he couldn't help adding, "You can trust me."

"Can I? You're just using me to get the information you need. I'm convenient. I have no illusion that you'll be happy to be rid of me when you no longer need me."

He was glad that her anger and annoyance were centered solely on him now. If she hadn't already come to that realization, she'd soon see that Catherine's friendship was genuine. He could be the focus for her anger if that was what she needed him to be.

"Our current working relationship is beneficial to both of us. An argument could be made that you are also using me in your attempt to prove your father was somehow acting under outside forces."

She glowered at him. "Fine," she said on a huff and turned to look out the window for the remainder of their carriage ride.

~

WORTHINGTON WASN'T HAPPY TO SEE HIM. When Brantford entered the small cell, he glanced at him from
where he was lying on the cot, then shifted onto his side
to stare at the wall.

"I see you haven't changed your mind about being
cooperative."

There was no response.

Brantford watched the other man as he spoke. "I
have information you'll want to know."

Worthington didn't reply, but by the way the older
man's shoulders stiffened, it was clear he was thinking
about his family. Worried about them. Brantford would
put that concern to good use.

He stood in the doorway but moved into the room
now, indicating to Rose, who waited in the hallway just
outside the door, that she should enter. He lifted a finger
to his lips, instructing her to remain silent as he closed
the door to the cell. The man guarding the room was
one he could trust, but even so, he'd given instructions
that the guard stand several feet away from the door so
he wouldn't overhear their conversation. Ellen would see
to it that he followed those instructions.

He nodded to Rose, who stepped farther into the
room. He didn't miss the way she was wringing her
hands, her lips pressed together in concern.

"Papa?"

That had an immediate reaction. Worthington
leaped from the bed and stared at his daughter in shock.

When his wild gaze swung back to him, Brantford could see real fear on the older man's face.

"She shouldn't be here."

"I quite agree. However, we appear to be at an impasse, and you know your daughter. She wants to help."

"You don't understand—" Worthington ran his hands over his thinning hair, agitation evident in the shaky movement.

Rose looked to Brantford, and when he nodded, she went to her father. "Everything is going to be fine, Papa. Tell us what you know and we'll find the real culprit and have you out of here."

Worthington dropped his hands and glared at Brantford. "You know exactly what you're doing by bringing her here with you. Anyone who sees the two of you together…" He gave his head a sharp shake. "Her life was already in danger, but this? If anything happens to her, I'll kill you myself."

Brantford raised a brow, feigning a detachment he was far from feeling. Fortunately, his reputation worked wonders and he didn't have to do anything beyond that to have the other man believing he really didn't care about Rose's life.

"Sweetheart," Worthington said, turning to his daughter, "please listen to me. The Tower is no place for a young woman. There is no hope for me now. You need to distance yourself from me. In time, all this will blow over and you'll marry." He raised a shaking hand, cupped his daughter's cheek, then dropped it again.

Brantford should have been moved by the concern on the older man's face. Instead, all he could feel was anger.

"Miss Hardwick might not have to wait long at all. Lord Standish has approached Overlea, whom you know has taken her into his home, to court your daughter."

Worthington stumbled back, all color draining from his face. "No…"

"Is something amiss? I thought that was what you wanted. Someone to give your daughter his name and protection. I know you were hoping Lord Kerrick would be that man, but…" He raised a shoulder in a casual shrug. "Beggars can't be choosers. Besides, Standish is wealthy enough."

"You bastard." Worthington's fists clenched, and he suspected Rose's presence was the only thing keeping Worthington from trying to hit him.

Rose flinched, but to her credit she didn't say a word. Brantford didn't take his eyes from the other man, who was struggling with this new turn of events.

Brantford knew he had won when the man slumped onto his cot.

"Fine, you win," he said, his voice low. "I'll tell you what I know, but not in front of my daughter."

Brantford nodded and turned to Rose. "Miss Hardwick?"

He could tell Rose didn't want to leave, but she nodded in reply. After bending to give her father a quick hug—one that appeared to shatter the older man's resolve even further—she left the dark cell, closing the door firmly behind her.

"She's not safe—"

"I have two of my most trusted people right outside that door. No harm will come to her."

Worthington swallowed and looked away, defeat outlined in every bone of his body. "I don't have much information. Not enough for you to convict the man who is responsible for selling secrets to the French. But I'll tell you everything I know in exchange for your promise to keep Rose safe."

Brantford nodded and lowered himself into the lone chair in the room.

"You do realize it is too late to keep her out of this? I tried but failed. If Standish has his way, he *will* kill her."

Brantford remained still, but he knew Worthington was correct. He refused to entertain the notion that he might just have signed Rose's death warrant.

"She'll be safe. You have my word."

Worthington searched his face before nodding. "If it becomes necessary, promise me you'll offer her your name."

Brantford reeled at what Rose's father was suggesting. "I can't marry her…"

"You may not have to. Heaven knows, the last thing I want is for my daughter to be married to a cold fish like you. But I've heard the rumors. I know how ruthless you can be. I also know you've never raised a hand to a woman in your life. If you can't keep her safe any other way—if it's no longer sufficient for her simply to remain under the protection of the Marquess of Overlea—you must promise me that you will offer her the protection of your name and all the resources that come with it."

"What do you know of my resources?" Brantford asked, his curiosity genuine.

Worthington shook his head. "Not much, I'm afraid. But Standish does. He's dropped hints about you. I believe he knows a good deal. And if I'm not mistaken, I think he fears you."

Brantford's mouth tightened before he replied. "He should."

Worthington nodded. "You'll give me your word?"

Brantford allowed the question to hang in the air, but there was never any doubt that he would agree to Worthington's one condition. Rose Hardwick had dropped hints about having feelings for some unnamed man, but she might very well have to put those feelings aside.

"I'll do everything in my power to keep her safe. That includes marrying her, should the need arise."

Worthington extended his hand and Brantford shook it. He spared a moment to wonder why his promise didn't leave him unsettled but pushed the thought aside and waited for the other man to begin.

"Since you've already guessed, I can confirm the man at the center of this is Standish. You need to keep him away from Rose."

"I know that you confessed to keep her and Lady Worthington safe. But you can't expect me to believe you're completely innocent."

"Of treason, yes. Of being the worst sort of fool, no."

Brantford leaned back in his chair, arms folded across his chest, and took careful note of everything about the man before him. "Tell me what happened."

Worthington shook his head. "Standish knew of my friendship with Admiral Heddington and guessed that I might be privy to information about the movements of our naval fleet. He cornered me at the inn near my estate, which I visit occasionally, and we started drinking. I thought he was just being friendly. It never occurred to me to wonder why he would be in a small village in Norfolk. By the end of the evening, I was completely foxed. I didn't even realize I'd told him anything until he paid me a visit after I arrived in London with my family. He thanked me for letting him know about the movements of the British fleet. Told me that Napoleon rewarded his informants handsomely and that my payment was already in my bank account."

Worthington looked away. "I didn't believe him. I thought he was having one over on me. But I was able to confirm that a large amount of money had been deposited in my account. And the worst of it is that I don't know what information I might have given him. It's possible I told him nothing and he was trying to coerce me into revealing something of value, but..." He gave his head a defeated shake. "I can't remember that evening."

"You kept the money."

Worthington clenched his jaw. "Yes, but I never

touched it. I didn't know what to do. I wanted to return it, but I didn't want anyone to connect me to Standish or his actions."

Brantford narrowed his eyes. "And you continued to pass on secrets."

Worthington shook his head. "No. Absolutely not."

"Now I think you're trying to play me for the fool. There was more than one deposit into your bank account."

"Don't you think I don't know that? I wasn't stupid enough to touch another drop after that first incident, but Standish was trying to force me to comply. Hounding me. Telling me no one would believe I hadn't been complicit from the start."

"And then he threatened your family."

Worthington sprang up from the cot, paced to the door, then back. Brantford continued to watch him.

"Yes, damn it. The blackguard threatened to kill my wife. He assured me he'd take more time with Rose before granting her the release of death." His eyes were wild, his breathing uneven. "You have to keep him away from them."

Brantford waved a hand to indicate Worthington resume his seat. Only when the other man complied did he speak.

"Tell me everything you know about Standish and his connections."

CHAPTER 7

*R*OSE'S NERVES WERE STRETCHED TAUT during the return carriage ride. As expected, Ellen, who was now acting as her maid, sat by her side. But she hadn't anticipated that Brantford would also be accompanying them.

He'd been tight-lipped when he exited her father's cell, saying very little. Now he sat opposite her again, but he'd resisted all efforts on her part to learn what her father had told him. She would have listened outside the cell, though she doubted she would have heard much since the door appeared to be quite thick, but Ellen had drawn her away. She'd spent the next fifteen minutes waiting with Brantford's sister and the guard several feet down the hall, feeling as though she were about to crawl out of her skin.

As the carriage slowed in front of the fashionable address, Rose turned away from the window.

"You have to tell me something. Anything."

Brantford's expression didn't change, and she had to resist the almost overwhelming urge to shake him. How could he just sit there, as still as a statue, when he knew how much this meant to her? She'd allowed him to use her in his quest for information, and the fear on her father's face when he'd seen them together had almost broken her heart. The least he could do was give her a tiny morsel of information.

She'd almost given up, knowing the effort was futile, when he finally spoke.

"Ellen, please wait for us outside the carriage."

Her breath caught in her throat as she watched Brantford's sister cast a curious glance in his direction before she moved to follow his instructions. She closed the carriage door behind her to give them privacy.

"Much as I would like to ease your mind, I can't tell you what I learned today."

Was that sympathy she glimpsed in his eyes? No, she must be imagining it. "Can't or won't?"

"Does it matter?"

The urge to shake him returned. "Can you at least tell me if Papa told you anything that will help him?"

He considered her request, and it was all she could do to wait. When she realized she was holding her breath, she released it with a soft sigh.

"Your faith in your father isn't entirely misplaced."

It wasn't much, but it told her everything she needed to know. Papa wasn't guilty of treason. She had clung to that belief with every fiber of her being, but she wasn't a fool. There had always been a slight chance she was wrong.

She reached out and placed a hand over one of Brantford's, where it rested on his knee. "Thank you."

Shock, and a small thrill of awareness, went through her when he turned his hand over and clasped hers.

"Promise me you won't go out without Ellen and at least one of the men I've added to the staff. I'd rather you didn't go out at all, but if I've learned anything, it's that you'll do exactly as you want."

She was stunned to see his concern for her written plainly on his face. She squeezed his hand. "I give you my word."

Silence stretched between them for several seconds before he nodded and released her hand. She missed that small measure of intimacy but said nothing before exiting the carriage.

She noticed the small smile on Ellen's face, but Brantford's sister said nothing as they entered the house. Only when the door to the town house was closed behind them did she hear the sound of carriage wheels on the cobblestones as the conveyance pulled away from the house.

Ellen nodded to the footman stationed just inside the door. He was one of Brantford's men. Another midway down the hall and a third was by the door leading out into the back garden. She wondered just how many men had been added to Overlea's staff and had to push down her guilt at the turmoil she'd caused.

Brantford had told her Catherine was also in danger

from Lord Standish. Whether or not she resided with them, the marquess would have needed to increase his security. Lord Kerrick knew of the danger the other man posed to his betrothed's safety and would have seen to it.

Catherine came rushing into the entrance hall, and Rose felt a pang of dismay looking at her. They hadn't known each other long, but Rose had taken an instant liking to her and had gone out of her way to befriend Catherine. She hated to think her friend had reciprocated only because she wanted to help Lord Kerrick gain information about her father's activities.

Catherine smiled at Ellen and turned to face Rose. "I promised myself that I wouldn't pry, and I mean to stick to that promise. I just wanted to make sure you were fine after your visit with your father."

Rose hadn't told Catherine the real reason for her visit, but her friend did know that Brantford had escorted her instead of Kerrick. And since Catherine was a smart woman, she'd have guessed that something important had taken place.

That was one of the reasons Rose had liked her immediately. Catherine wasn't like many of the debutantes who'd come out that season, concerned only about her hair and the cut of her dress.

She didn't want to have this conversation, but there was no point in putting it off. "Can we speak privately?"

Catherine's brow creased. "Of course. Would you like to come into the drawing room?"

Rose nodded, then turned to Ellen. "Thank you for coming with me today. I'll let you know if I need you again."

The other woman gave her a brisk nod but didn't leave right away. Rose could feel her speculative gaze on her as she followed Catherine the short distance to the drawing room and closed the door behind them.

Catherine waited for Rose to speak first, clearly unwilling to press her for details she might not want to share. Rose had always appreciated that about her.

Rose began to pace, trying to ignore the look of concern on her friend's face.

Catherine moved to the settee. "You don't have to tell me anything about what happened today. I understand completely if it's too difficult for you."

Rose turned to face her, needing to have this conversation over with as soon as possible. The uncertainty about Catherine's friendship was killing her.

"Is our acquaintance genuine, Catherine?"

If the way Catherine's mouth gaped open was any indication, she was truly surprised. But did her reaction stem from her surprise at having her friendship questioned or at having her ruse discovered?

"I… What? What do you mean by that? Of course it's genuine. Why would you think it wasn't?"

Rose dropped into a chair, hating that she felt guilty for the hurt in her friend's face. But she was hurt too.

"I know your betrothed was investigating my father. I never understood why he was courting me when it was clear that he preferred you. It didn't make sense that he was acting on the wishes of his parents and mine."

Catherine leaned back and closed her eyes. "I'd hoped you wouldn't learn about that."

"Well, I did, and it explains so much. Such as why you, the woman who wanted him for herself, would form a friendship with the woman he was courting. Were you trying to ply me for information?"

The guilt in Catherine's eyes when she opened them was answer enough. Rose stood. "You were."

"Ugh, I am so bad at this. Why did I think I should involve myself?"

Rose turned to leave the room, but Catherine sprang up and grabbed her hand. Reluctantly, Rose allowed Catherine to pull her down next to her on the settee.

"No, I won't allow you to leave until I've told you everything."

"What more is there to say?" Rose didn't know how she would be able to stand the sting of this betrayal. To discover that the one friend she'd thought she had left wasn't her friend after all was more than she could bear.

"I was a silly, ignorant child when I visited you that first day at your house. You remember that, right? I thought that if I got close to you, I could help Kerrick come to the end of his investigation more quickly. But you pulled me into your confidence right away. Used me to dodge all those men who'd called on you and we escaped to the garden." Catherine smiled, but her eyes were bright with unshed tears. "You threw me completely off with your welcome. And I discovered very quickly that I enjoyed your company very much."

Rose really didn't want to ask the next question, but she had to know. "Were you and Kerrick laughing at me behind my back?"

Catherine's eyes widened. "No! Absolutely not! We never poked fun at you. In fact, the opposite was true. Once I came to know you, I hated that your father was under suspicion. I wanted nothing more than for Kerrick to find information that would show Brantford he was wrong about him." Her hand flew to her mouth. "I've said too much. You weren't supposed to know that."

Rose nodded. So Kerrick had been acting on Brantford's orders. She wasn't surprised.

"Rose, my friendship is real. I will do anything you need me to do. Anything." She dashed a tear from her eye as she spoke.

Catherine wasn't that good of an actress. If she were, she would have been able to conceal her feelings for Lord Kerrick. Catherine would have been able to get more information from her if so many of their outings hadn't centered around Rose's schemes to bring Kerrick and Catherine together. And now that she thought of it, Catherine had never once pried for information about her father.

"I believe you," Rose said, tears coming to her own eyes. "You understand why I had to ask."

"Of course," Catherine said, gripping her in a hug.

"I hate that you're going through this. I wish there was something I could do to make it better."

Rose pulled back and gave her a tremulous smile. "Just continue to be my friend. I couldn't get through this if I didn't know you were at my side."

Catherine nodded, the tears falling freely as she pulled her into another hug.

CHAPTER 8

*B*RANTFORD COULDN'T REMEMBER the last time he'd been out in the field. For several years now, he'd collected information solely through his many associates.

He'd considered asking Kerrick to perform tonight's particular mission. It wouldn't have taken much convincing since Catherine was still in danger from Standish. But in the end, he decided he needed to observe Standish himself.

Which was why he now found himself in a seamy gambling hell by the docks that his quarry was known to frequent. Standish would have heard about his and Rose's visit to the Tower and would know exactly why Brantford was there.

His thoughts kept returning to the promise he'd given Worthington, which was another reason why he'd decided to undertake tonight's activity. He needed to ascertain just how much danger Rose was in. If he'd learned anything over the years, it was never to ignore his instincts, and right now they were telling him it was possible he might need to fulfill his promise to Rose's father.

He sat with his back to the wall, facing the entrance. The position would allow him to watch Standish unobserved when he arrived.

A few men had glanced his way, but no one bothered him. He wasn't the only man sitting alone, but he was the only one not in his cups.

He didn't have to wait long before Standish strode, alone, into the dark establishment. Brantford had entertained a vague hope the man would be accompanied by at least one of his associates. He knew they existed since Standish was too well informed to be acting alone. At the very least, the man had his own network of informants.

Brantford remained where he was seated near the back of the establishment, which afforded him the opportunity to study his prey before he was spotted.

Standish was about the same age as him. They hadn't been classmates at Oxford, and Brantford had assumed the man had gone to Cambridge. But thanks to Kerrick, he knew now that Standish had never attended university because his father had sent him abroad to shield him from the consequences of having murdered his cousin.

Outwardly, Standish was the very epitome of a man of his station. His brown hair was kept short, as was the current mode, and he took great care to flaunt his wealth through his attention to fashion. Beau Brummell himself could take lessons from the man.

He'd noticed that Standish gave off a sinister air that made others nervous around him. Brantford had witnessed it on more than one occasion, but of course he'd never really cared one way or the other.

That was before the man became a threat to Rose.

Standish's eyes swept across the room. He started toward one group but stopped and changed direction when he spotted him. Brantford took note of the men he'd been about to join—he knew many of the patrons present this evening. He had a few of his own men interspersed throughout the room and knew they'd provide him with the names of those in that group he didn't already know.

His attention focused on Standish. He half expected the man to leave, but it appeared Standish was willing to play the game. He stalked toward Brantford, not bothering to hide his amusement, and lowered himself into the other seat at the small table.

"This is a surprise," Standish said, his eyes sweeping over the table and no doubt taking in the fact that Brantford wasn't drinking. "Though I must say, not an unpleasant one."

"I found myself bored this evening."

Standish smiled, a gruesome affair that threatened Brantford's composure. "Excellent," he said. "I've long wanted to play you, but everyone knows you never gamble. Tell me, are you really that bad? Surely you can afford to lighten your pockets every once in a while."

Brantford looked the other man over slowly, knowing how much Standish would hate the implied censure in his gaze. "Quite the opposite. It's tiring winning all the time. No challenge."

Standish's jaw tightened, his eyes flashing briefly in annoyance. "I think you'll find me a worthy opponent."

Brantford looked away, forcing Standish to wait for his response. It was a small thing, but he could almost feel the weight of the other man's glare. After several moments, he raised a hand, making a casual motion to one of the barmaids. A pack of cards appeared within seconds.

Standish opened the pack and began to shuffle. "It will be a pleasant change to play someone who isn't already completely foxed. Piquet?"

Brantford gave the man an abbreviated nod, watching as he handled the cards with the finesse of a sharp. He knew then that he wouldn't intentionally throw this game. Most men would be too wrapped up in their victory to know—or care—how they'd won. Pair that with a few drinks, and they'd be an open book. But Standish wasn't a fool. He'd know if Brantford lost by design, especially since he too wasn't drinking. Nothing would be gained.

Better to work on the insight Worthington had given him that morning—that Standish feared him. Frustration at being unable to best him might work where empty victories wouldn't.

The task proved more difficult than he'd anticipated. He shouldn't have been surprised to discover Standish was skilled at cards. Not as skilled as he, however. After his third loss, Standish threw the cards down in disgust.

"You really do think you're better than the rest of us," Standish uttered, a dangerous gleam in his eye.

"Three hands would seem to bear that out. Perhaps one day I'll meet my match. But we both know that won't be you."

Standish stood, his chair scraping back in protest at the abrupt motion. He leaned forward, towering over Brantford, who moved not a muscle.

"I'm going to wipe that superior look from your face. Don't think I don't know that the Worthington chit is under your protection. The young swains are already lining up, waiting for the opportunity to offer her carte blanche when Overlea sets her loose. But when I'm through with her, there won't be anything left for them."

Brantford dropped his facade then, allowing the other man to see the cold, deadly heat he knew was in his eyes. He wanted nothing more than to tear Standish limb from limb for even thinking about Rose. Satisfaction flowed through him when he saw the doubt that entered the other man's expression.

"If you go near Rose Hardwick, it will be the very last thing you do."

Rallying, Standish tossed out an eager "Let the games begin, Brantford" before turning and striding from the hell.

Brantford had to sit there for a full minute before he was able to get his temper back in check.

He made eye contact with his men, signaling that

they should concentrate on the group seated at the table Standish had been heading toward and then stood to leave.

Standish had made a grave error that night in threatening Rose Hardwick. Time would tell whether he'd actually live to see the gallows or if Brantford was going kill him with his bare hands.

BRANTFORD LOOKED UP from the report he was reading when the door to his study swung open. His sister sauntered into the room and sat primly in his guest chair.

"You sent for me, Lord B?"

Brantford closed the file and set it aside, working to tamp down his annoyance. His thoughts had circled around his conversation with Standish the previous evening and he hadn't been able to concentrate on the documents. He'd have to try later to read the file. After everything was settled.

"Is that necessary when it's just the two of us?"

She lifted one shoulder. "All right, Brantford." At his frown, she continued. "You may be my younger brother, but you ceased being Lucien a long time ago. I can't even remember the last time I caught a glimpse of that sweet little boy."

Brantford rose and moved to the sideboard. He poured his sister a glass of sherry and for himself a small measure of brandy. He needed to keep his wits about him and couldn't afford more than that.

His sister's words brought up unpleasant memories he'd tried his best to forget. That sweet little boy she missed had died a long time ago, crushed under the unrelenting demands his father had made of his heir. He couldn't begin to imagine why she'd bring the past up now, and he wasn't about to ask.

He handed Ellen her glass and resumed his seat behind the desk.

His sister frowned. "You work far too much. You couldn't step outside your study to receive me?"

"If memory serves, you barged in here and made yourself at home. Besides, this isn't a social call."

His sister sighed and took a sip of her sherry. "No, I suppose it isn't. I told you I'd keep you informed of Rose's movements. She hasn't left the house since your visit to the Tower yesterday, and nothing untoward has occurred. No attempts to break into the house, no unusual correspondence."

Brantford had to restrain himself from downing the small amount of brandy he'd allowed himself in one gulp. Even then, half was gone when he lowered the glass and faced his sister.

"In exchange for his information, Worthington extracted a promise from me to watch over his daughter."

Ellen gave a small shrug. "He should have realized you've been doing that since the beginning."

"Not quite. He wanted me to promise him that I'd give her the protection of my name."

That got his sister's attention. She almost choked on her sherry.

Ellen placed the glass on his desk and glared at him. "You could have waited for me to finish taking a sip before springing that on me."

Brantford didn't hide his amusement. "Yes, but it's always so much fun to catch you off guard. It happens so rarely."

"So." Ellen leaned back and glared at her brother. "Worthington made you promise to wed Rose. And you agreed. That doesn't seem like you."

"Not quite." Brantford resisted the urge to down the rest of his drink by placing the glass on his desk. "He only insisted I do so if it became necessary."

"And is it? Necessary?"

"I didn't think so when I spoke to him. I thought I had things well in hand, but I ran into Standish last night."

Ellen's eyes gleamed with interest. "And?"

"And he threatened her. He didn't come right out and say he was planning to kill her, but that was the substance of his statement."

Ellen gave her head a small shake of her head. "Leave it to you to make an already bad situation worse."

Brantford refused to rise to the bait. "We both know her life was already in danger. Why else would Worthington admit to a crime he didn't commit?"

"Don't try to make light of this. You said yourself you didn't think you'd have to marry the poor girl, but now you're saying that after running into Standish, you do. Therefore, you made the situation worse."

Brantford narrowed his eyes. "Standish knows I'm closing in. If Miss Hardwick had retired to the country with her mother, she'd be safe right now. Standish would have no need to pay her any attention. She put herself in this position by remaining in London and insisting on visiting her father. And yes, I used her desire to help her father to my advantage yesterday, but it was always going to happen. Standish couldn't very well ignore a potential leak."

He downed the rest of the brandy, hating that his sister could rile him up so easily. "What are you smiling at?" he asked when he noticed she no longer appeared angry.

"You want to marry her."

His stomach hollowed at the certainty in her voice. Did he want to marry Rose Hardwick?

It only took him a moment to realize that he did. She was temptation itself. When he was around her, he had to hold himself severely in check. Force himself not to betray just how much she affected him when the very opposite was true. He noticed everything about her. He'd never admit it to his sister, however. Nor would he let Rose know she held such power over him.

"My feelings are irrelevant."

Ellen released a frustrated sigh. "Of course they are. Excuse me for thinking otherwise." She took another sip of her sherry before asking, "Is Worthington innocent?"

"Not entirely. He did pass information on to Standish, but apparently it happened only once and when he was in his cups. I'm inclined to believe him."

"The poor fool. Will you be able to do anything for him?"

That was the question really. He honestly didn't know. "If I can get Standish, maybe. I'd have to prove that it happened only that one time. I'm not sure if I'll be able to do that. Even if I find concrete evidence that Standish is the person selling secrets to the French, I'm not sure I'd be able to get him to admit he played Worthington for a fool."

Ellen frowned. "Maybe if we threaten someone he cares about in turn? It worked for Worthington."

"Standish doesn't have a heart. I'm beginning to think he belongs in Bedlam. I doubt he's capable of caring for anyone." He paused, wondering if Standish had met his real mother when the old earl had sent him to the continent, but discarded the thought almost immediately. In all likelihood, he blamed her for abandoning him and wouldn't lift a finger to help her if he thought her life in danger.

"Well, I see I'll get nothing more out of you," Ellen said, standing. She placed her unfinished glass of sherry on the desk. "Should we expect you later today?"

Brantford nodded. The sooner he had Rose under his protection, the better.

CHAPTER 9

*A*S THE CARRIAGE WHEELS clattered along the cobblestone streets later that afternoon, Brantford laid his head against the thick squab and closed his eyes. He'd been unable to shake the awareness that silent eyes were watching his every move since leaving his town house. Of course, that was normally true. He couldn't go anywhere without curious onlookers staring at him. Some tried to hide their curiosity, but many watched him openly. The more remote he became, the worse they gawked.

Normally he could shake off that awareness, refusing to allow it to affect his actions or his mood. But not that afternoon.

Since the matter of his wedding to Rose Hardwick couldn't be postponed, he'd visited Doctors Commons to procure a special license right after speaking with his sister. The archbishop hadn't raised a brow after learning the reason for his visit. He supposed the man had seen more than one elusive member of the *ton* enter his office over the years. But Brantford wasn't quite so composed once he had the license in his possession. For the first time in years, he was feeling out of sorts, as though the very ground beneath his feet was shifting and each step threatened to send him tumbling.

He flexed his fingers and shifted his shoulders as the carriage drew ever closer to Overlea's home, trying to work out muscles that had become tense, and told himself things would go back to normal once he was done with this task. Marriage was a momentous change of state, and it was normal to feel a small amount of... something. He refused to name it as anxiety. Or anticipation. Whatever was wrong with him, he'd work through it and push it into the background where it belonged. Nothing had to change. Many men went about their daily routine, rarely even seeing their wives.

Although it would be a shame to marry Rose Hardwick and then deposit her somewhere he'd rarely have occasion to visit.

Gritting his teeth in annoyance at the wayward thought, he forced his mind to go over what he'd learned so far about Standish and what steps he needed to take next. He and Rose needed to pay a visit to her mother, and this time the woman wouldn't be able to turn him away. He tried not to think about the trip to Essex, during which they'd need to share the intimate confines of his carriage.

Worthington hadn't told him much. He'd kept written notes about each of his conversations with Standish though, and Brantford needed to get his hands on them. Apparently he'd asked his wife to keep them safe. He insisted that the documents were sealed and that his wife wouldn't have read them. Brantford hoped that was true. If Standish even suspected that Lady Worthington had knowledge about their conversations, she wouldn't be safe anywhere.

Worthington had also told him that he'd used his friendship with Admiral Heddington to unearth some information of his own about Standish. What, the man wouldn't say. Only that he'd planned to use it after the season was over and Rose successfully wed.

The admiral wasn't currently in England or Brantford would have contacted him directly instead of having to chase down these hidden documents. But if the admiral knew anything about Standish's crimes as a young man before his father had sent him away, Brantford would find a way to leverage that proof against him. The privilege of peerage didn't extend to murder. Standish could still be hanged for that crime even if they couldn't connect him to the charge of treason. If he couldn't prove Worthington's innocence, they'd both hang. He hated thinking about how distraught Rose would be if that happened.

Brantford sprang from the carriage when it drew to a halt, eager to get this task over with. He'd sent word ahead that he needed to speak to Overlea, so when he entered the town house, the butler informed him that the marquess was waiting for him in the library.

Feeling eyes on him once again, Brantford halted

and glanced up. Rose stood, frozen, at the top of the stairs. Her hand had fluttered to her chest, her eyes wide with surprise. It appeared no one had told her he would be paying a call.

Ignoring the unease that was now a constant companion since he'd spoken to Standish the night before, he offered her an abbreviated bow and followed the butler to the library.

Overlea stood and extended his hand when he entered. Brantford couldn't help but recall their meeting the previous fall, when Overlea had looked deathly ill. Of course, that was to be expected when one was being poisoned. Unlike with Overlea's father and brother before him, however, the culprit had been caught in time and he was now back to his normal self. Brantford had played a small role in finding the person responsible, and he knew he could count on the assistance of the man before him.

"You're looking hale and hearty," Brantford said.

Overlea's lips twisted in a semblance of a smile. "That was a nasty business. I'm just glad it's over and that gossip about the incident hasn't spread."

Brantford tipped his head in acknowledgment of the unvoiced thanks. "We aim to serve."

A sound at the door had Brantford turning to see Kerrick sauntering into the room.

"I hope you don't mind," Overlea said, "but when I received word you wanted to speak with me, I thought Kerrick should join us. He knows more about this whole situation than I. I only know that Miss Hardwick needs someone to protect her, and as she is a close friend of Catherine's, I'm more than happy to provide that protection."

Brantford hid his annoyance as he spoke to Kerrick. "For a man who wanted nothing more to do with this matter, you seem to be deeply embroiled in it."

Kerrick smiled. "It's good to see you too, old chap. It's been what… one day? Two?"

Brantford ignored the man and turned back to Overlea. He'd hoped not to have to do this in front of Kerrick, but apparently, as was ever his lot in life, he'd have to deal with having his actions scrutinized yet again.

"Would you care for something?" Overlea asked.

Brantford gave a sharp shake of his head. "This will be a short call. I'm here to let you know that there has been a change in plans with respect to Miss Hardwick."

Overlea raised a brow in answer to his statement, but of course Kerrick couldn't remain silent on the subject.

"What do you mean by 'a change of plans'? As far as I know, Rose has no intention of joining her mother in the country, and she can hardly return to her town house alone."

Brantford tossed an assessing glare at the other man, wondering briefly when Kerrick had become immune to his censure.

"No, of course not," Brantford said. "If you'll allow me to continue?"

Kerrick crossed his arms over his chest. "By all means."

Brantford turned back to Overlea. "I've spoken to Worthington, and we've agreed that Miss Hardwick needs more protection than you can provide her here."

"With all the men you've added to my staff, the only place more secure than my home at the moment is the Tower." He frowned briefly. "You're not intended to keep her there, are you?"

"Of course not," Brantford said. "Gone are the days of housing royalty or other nobles in the Tower for their safety."

"Then where will she go?" Overlea asked.

Brantford studiously ignored Kerrick, hating that he was witnessing this moment given the man's recent encouragements about Rose, and continued. "She'll come with me. I've decided that the only way to keep her safe is to give her the protection of my name."

Silence descended after his statement. He'd expected Overlea to be surprised by his announcement, but instead he saw only speculation on the other man's face. "Indeed. That does seem to be the best route forward."

"Devil take it," Kerrick interrupted. "Is that all you're going to say? You're going to marry Rose just to keep her safe?"

"You offered to do the same not that long ago. And if memory serves, you had every intention of going through with it to keep Rose and her mother safe."

Kerrick pointed a finger at him. "That's not the same thing at all, and you know it. Rose and I were maneuvered into a compromising position, and I had no choice but to announce we were betrothed so she wouldn't be ruined."

Brantford raised a brow and waited, unwilling to explain himself to Kerrick. He knew the other man would get to the logical conclusion of this argument on his own.

"You're infuriating, Brantford. You can at least admit you have feelings for Rose."

Brantford somehow kept himself from snarling at the other man. Every time Kerrick used Rose's Christian name, it was a reminder of just how close they had become.

Instead, he lifted a shoulder in a casual shrug. "For the sake of expediency, it only makes sense that I keep Miss Hardwick close. As my wife, I can protect her where Overlea cannot. I can also stop the unseemly rumors that are swirling about concerning her."

"You've heard those?" Overlea asked. "Never mind, of course you have. There is quite a bit of money wagered in the betting books at White's about who will be the first to have Rose for their mistress. I, for one, am glad she'll be avoiding that fate."

"Indeed," Brantford said, although inside he was seething. He'd have to stop by White's to see who had added their names to that wager.

"About that," Kerrick said, reaching into his coat pocket and producing a piece of paper. He held it out to Brantford. "Here you go."

Brantford took it, a quick glance revealing it was a

list of names. Many of those names belonged to the young men who'd surrounded Rose wherever she went that season.

"I took the liberty of having a look at the betting book," Kerrick said. "That's a list of all the men who took part in that wager." Brantford looked at him, unable to hide his surprise, and Kerrick continued. "I thought you'd want to know."

"Yes. Thank you for this."

Overlea made a soft scoffing sound, and Brantford turned back to face him. "You wanted to add something to this discussion?"

"Not at all. I was just imagining all the ways you could make those young idiots suffer for their presumption."

"Indeed," Brantford said, allowing himself to share in the other man's amusement. "I can be quite imaginative."

Kerrick laughed out loud. "See, Nicholas," he said, turning to Overlea. "I told you he had feelings, much as he would have everyone believe that wasn't the case."

Brantford narrowed his eyes at the man, refusing to be provoked. Kerrick didn't so much as flinch.

"Chin up, old boy. It will hardly be a hardship—"

"Yes," Brantford said, cutting him off. He'd said much the same thing to Kerrick when he'd asked him, at the start of the season, to court Rose so he could get closer to Worthington to investigate him. It wasn't the first time Kerrick had repeated them in his mistaken belief that Brantford had tender feelings for Rose. "You can stop throwing my words back in my face now."

Instead of being put in his place, Kerrick seemed to take enjoyment from his annoyance, and Brantford cursed himself for rising to the other man's bait after all.

CHAPTER 10

*M*ORE THAN ANYTHING, ROSE HATED WAITING. Her parents had often chided her for her impatience, and right now she wished she'd made more of an effort to curb that flaw.

When Brantford had headed down the hallway, she'd wanted nothing more than to follow him and listen in on whatever conversation he was having with Catherine's brother-in-law.

To keep from being found with her ear pressed against a door, she went immediately in search of Catherine. Now they waited in the drawing room. Brantford would have to pass the room to leave the house. If he didn't come see her, Catherine assured her that she would ask Overlea what had taken place.

For surely something must have happened for Brantford to visit the marquess instead of her. Her mind whirled with all sorts of horrible possibilities. Perhaps even now they were trying to think of some way to break the bad news to her. She stared blindly out the window, taking in the quiet street outside.

She jumped when Catherine touched her shoulder. "Try not to worry. It might be nothing."

Rose gave her friend a wry smile. "That's easier said than done. Since this whole thing started, everything seems to have gone from bad to worse. I don't think I can take more bad news."

"It might not be bad. You said yourself that Lord Brantford told you your faith in your father wasn't misplaced. He might have discovered something that would prove his innocence."

"If that was the case, why would he be speaking to Lord Overlea and not to me?" She moved away from the window toward the door, then stopped. "It is taking everything in me not to listen in on their conversation. Do you think they're in the study? Maybe you could ask a footman. It won't seem so odd a question coming from you."

At the sound of voices and footsteps, Rose froze, nerves overcoming her. Catherine took her by the hand and led her to the settee, then tugged her down next to her. Rose didn't turn to thank her friend. Her gaze was riveted on the drawing room door as she wondered if Brantford would stop to speak with her.

The voices stopped just before three men entered the room. Rose frowned in confusion when she saw Kerrick. She'd seen Brantford arrive but hadn't realized that Catherine's betrothed was also present. He must have arrived when she'd gone in search of Catherine.

Lord Overlea bowed in their direction. "Miss Hardwick, Catherine. I hope you don't mind, but I have other business to attend to right now. Besides, my presence here is decidedly *de trop*."

Was that amusement she saw in his eyes as he took his leave? Rose had no doubt he was going in search of his wife, and she felt her nerves begin to settle. Catherine's brother-in-law wouldn't be amused if something bad had happened. He wasn't one to take pleasure in the misfortune of others.

But her curiosity was still firmly in place, especially when Kerrick made a comment about taking in the garden with Catherine. She didn't miss that he pulled the drawing room door closed behind them.

Before she knew what was happening, Rose found herself alone with Lord Brantford. He seemed more remote than ever this morning, and her nerves returned.

She rose swiftly to her feet. "What has happened?"

"Please," he said, sweeping a hand toward the settee.

Rose did as he asked, hating that she couldn't read the man. She expected him to take one of the other seats and let out a soft sound of surprise when he settled on the settee next to her, although he was careful to maintain a respectable distance.

She couldn't wait any longer. "Do you have news of Papa?"

"Nothing has changed with respect to you father."

Brantford's eyes went to her hands, which she realized were clutching the fabric of her dress. She relaxed her grip, forcing herself not to shake the elusive man sitting next to her.

"My nerves can't handle all this secrecy."

His eyes met hers then, and she saw a hint of amusement before he carefully masked it. That, more than anything else, helped to settle her fears.

"I'm here today not because of your father but because of you."

"Me?" She had no idea to what he could be referring. "I've already told you everything I know, which I'll admit isn't very much. I wish I did have more information."

"Again, you're assuming this has to do with what is happening to your father. But as I've already said, I'm here for you."

And just like that, her heart started pounding in her chest. The way he'd phrased that, it almost seemed... No, she was imagining things. Allowing her foolish infatuation with Brantford to make her see things that weren't there.

"I'm listening," she said, afraid to say more lest she betray herself in any way.

"After speaking to your father the other day and discovering some things on my own, I've come to realize that the danger to your life is very real."

Rose could only stare at him. Would Brantford lie to her about this to get her to join her mother in the country?

"I'm not leaving London," she said, annoyance flaring that they kept returning to this subject.

"No, of course not. Nor do I expect you to. But it has become clear that Overlea can't provide you with the protection you require."

He was talking in circles, dancing around something.

"Where do you expect me to go? Ellen told me that you've added men to the staff who can keep me safe. Catherine, as well, since we know Lord Standish was fixated on her. And I've already promised you that I won't leave the house on my own. This is the safest place in London for me to be."

Brantford's eyes seemed to bore into hers, the emotion in them one she couldn't decipher, and she was torn between turning away from him and bridging the small distance that separated them. It was with great difficulty that she waited for him to reply.

"You'd be safer with me."

Rose felt her mouth drop open, and she closed it with a snap. "What did you just say?"

"I can keep you safe."

She shook her head. "I know. That's why you've sent your sister to me and have men watching the house…" She was babbling. She knew it, but it seemed she was powerless to stop. "My imagination is running away with me. Please be plain, my lord. I know it must be difficult for you, but try to eschew all this secretive business you like to wrap yourself in."

One corner of his mouth lifted, and Rose felt her heart soar in response.

"I think I can do that. The safest place for you right now is under my personal protection. To do that, we need to get married. I've already procured a special license."

Rose sprang to her feet, and Brantford rose swiftly as well. She walked away from him, turning to face him again when several feet separated them.

"I'm sorry, but I think I misheard you. I thought… Did you just propose to me?"

Brantford inclined his head. "There is nothing wrong with your hearing."

She had to turn away again, her thoughts and emotions in turmoil. Brantford had proposed marriage to her. Brantford. The man she loved but who was impossible.

Only, he wasn't impossible any longer.

Logically, she knew he was only proposing to keep her safe. He didn't actually care for her.

But what if she could make him care? What better position from which to do that than by his side, as his wife?

"Miss Hardwick? Rose?"

Rose closed her eyes, the sound of her name spoken in that smooth, low voice almost more than she could handle.

She should protest. Tell him that it wasn't necessary that he sacrifice himself for her. She'd done the same thing for Kerrick not that long ago, after all.

But Kerrick had been in love with someone else. As had she… with the man who'd just proposed to her. Most marriages were based on much less. She could love him enough for the two of them and perhaps, in time, he'd come to see her as more than a responsibility.

She turned to face him, her mind made up but her heart still racing.

"Yes. I'll marry you."

CHAPTER 11

*B*RANTFORD SMILED AT HER THEN, one of his rare full smiles that made her feel as though her heart had stuttered.

It occurred to her that it would be a shame to be on the verge of having everything she wanted—her father's name cleared and about to wed the man for whom she'd long had a hopeless *tendre*—only to expire because her heart gave out.

"I'll take my leave of you now. I have a few favors to call in to make sure this happens seamlessly. Ellen will help you on this end, and come tomorrow, you'll be moving to my town house. Do you think that will pose a problem?"

Rose could only shake her head, suddenly bereft of words as he gave her a short bow before departing.

She remained rooted to the spot for several minutes, contemplating how quickly everything had changed for her. Again.

She and Brantford were going to be wed tomorrow. Given where her father was currently residing, as well as the fact that her mother was hiding in the country, she felt more than a spark of guilt for the happiness the thought gave her.

Her mother would hate what she'd call the unseemly haste with which her marriage was taking place. But since tongues were already wagging about her family, there was no point in waiting. Brantford wouldn't have proposed if he didn't think it necessary.

A shiver went through her just thinking about Lord Standish. She couldn't deny that there was something sinister about the man. His attentions had always been directed squarely at Catherine, but now it seemed he had shifted his focus to her.

Would he really harm her? Her father seemed to think so, and apparently so did Brantford if today's surprising turn of events was any indication. Logically, she knew she should be worried for her own safety, but she found it difficult to process the fact that everyone seemed to think she was in very real danger. It beggared belief that Lord Standish meant to harm her.

Rose didn't want to think about the speculation that would arise when others learned of their marriage. In a few months' time, when it became clear that Brantford hadn't married her because she was with child, the rumors would fade. With any luck, her father's name would also be cleared and they could go about putting this unpleasantness behind them.

She had to cling to that hope.

A flurry of activity in the hallway gave her enough time to brace herself for Catherine's return. Rose overheard her friend bidding her betrothed goodbye, and then she came hurrying into the drawing room. She rushed to Rose's side.

"Kerrick told me what was happening in here. Is it true? Did Lord Brantford really propose marriage?"

Rose could only nod in reply, still a little stunned by the dramatic turn of events herself.

"Did you accept?" Catherine asked, her eyes wide with curiosity.

"I did." Rose collapsed onto the settee. "We're going to be wed tomorrow."

Catherine gave a small squeal as she dropped next to Rose and enveloped her in a hug. She pulled back and Rose watched as her smile dimmed. "I'm happy for you, but I'm not sure if I'm supposed to be. Tell me that you're happy about this too. I know that you care for Lord Brantford."

Rose sighed. "Heaven help me, but I am. I know the reason for his proposal isn't ideal, but I can't help feeling hopeful about the future. Is that ridiculous?"

Catherine shook her head. "Absolutely not. I only hope that he knows how fortunate he is to have you."

Rose's lips twisted. "He's marrying me to keep me safe."

Catherine's voice lowered. "Louisa and Nicholas also wed for practical reasons, and look at how well that turned out. He's utterly devoted to her."

Rose had witnessed the same thing about the

marquess and his wife. She knew that her own parents' marriage had been arranged, and they also cared for one another. She suspected that was one of the reasons why her mother had felt so betrayed by her father's actions.

"We need to prepare for tomorrow," Catherine said. "Do you have a dress?"

"I'm sure I have something I can wear. It isn't going to be a big affair, so perhaps one of my gowns?"

Ellen swept into the room then, drawing their attention. "A little bird told me that someone is in need of a dress for her wedding."

Rose sighed. "It appears that everyone knew about my upcoming nuptials before me."

"I didn't," Catherine said. "Though I was probably learning about it at the same time you were."

"Since I had a little advance notice, I took the liberty of selecting a few dresses from which you can choose."

Rose could only stare at the woman who was posing as her maid. "Just how long have you known about this?"

Ellen's smile was enigmatic. "Since this morning. But it's amazing what one can accomplish when they use Lord Brantford's name. It doesn't hurt that he hasn't set any limits on what we can spend."

Catherine shook her head. "Who are you? You came out nowhere, and now we learn that Lord Brantford is confiding his secrets in you?"

Rose needed to change the subject quickly. She hadn't told anyone about Ellen's true identity. If the woman had wanted it known she was Brantford's sister, she wouldn't have gone through the effort to disguise her appearance and attempt to look older.

"Never mind," Rose said, rising. "We have a dress to choose. Would you like to help me, Catherine?"

Her friend grinned. "You won't be able to pry me from your side."

Rose locked arms with her, and together the trio of women proceeded up to her room. If she was going to get through the hours until her wedding, she would need to concentrate on the task at hand. She couldn't allow herself to get distracted wondering about her future with Brantford. She'd deal with him after they were married.

DESPITE ADMONISHING HERSELF not to dwell on things she couldn't control, thoughts of her upcoming wedding kept Rose from falling asleep for some time after she retired. Ellen had selected a variety of simple, elegant dresses, and Rose had finally settled on one that was light blue. It offset her fair coloring and chestnut-colored hair nicely but wasn't covered in ruffles or lace. Brantford was marrying her for practical reasons, and the last thing she wanted was to act as though she were a foolish romantic.

Even if she felt that way deep inside.

Morning came all too quickly with a very different Ellen waking her. She could scarce believe the beautiful blonde was the same woman who'd posed as her maid, even though she knew Brantford's sister had been wearing makeup to make herself appear older. She hadn't suspected that Ellen had also done something to her figure, which was now as slim as hers.

Ellen insisted on helping her dress despite Rose's protests. "I'm the same woman who's been helping you over the past few days," she said, brushing off her concerns.

When she finally emerged from her bedroom, Catherine was waiting for her in the hallway. After a quick hug and encouraging words about the future from her friend—as well as a meaningful glance in Ellen's direction that told her Catherine would be demanding to know the story behind the mysterious woman at some point—she was whisked away by Ellen. She wasn't surprised that two burly footmen escorted them to their carriage. Catherine and her sister, Lady Overlea, also found themselves similarly escorted to a second carriage. Outriders rode alongside the two carriages, drawing the attention of onlookers en route.

Overlea's carriage sported his crest, but the one in which Rose and Ellen rode had no such embellishment. Rose made sure to keep her face turned away from the window, hating the attention they were attracting.

The ride to the chapel was a short one. Rose had always dreamed of having a grand wedding, but of course this hurried event would only have a handful of guests.

A wave of sadness swept over her when Lord

Overlea offered her his arm to escort her down the aisle, but she forced it back. If she was going to make it through the day, she couldn't allow herself to dwell on the fact that neither of her parents were present to see her wed. Instead, she'd draw strength from the people around her.

Her gaze focused on where Brantford stood at the top of the aisle, facing the altar, as she made her way to his side. It took her a moment to realize she didn't know the dark-haired man at his side. She'd assumed Lord Kerrick would be acting as Brantford's witness, just as Catherine was acting as hers. Whoever the man was, she'd no doubt be seeing more of him in future if he was friends with her soon-to-be husband.

She had another moment of surprise when she realized Brantford had arranged for a bishop to conduct the ceremony.

When she finally reached the top of the aisle, Brantford turned and smiled at her. Her thoughts scattered, and she barely heard what the bishop was saying. When it came time to repeat her vows, she tripped over her words. Brantford's gaze was steady, but she caught a flicker of something in his expression. Concern, perhaps? She couldn't really tell because it was gone so quickly.

He took her hand and slid a ring onto her fourth finger, saying in that delightfully rich voice of his, "With this ring I thee wed, with my body I thee worship, and with all my worldly goods I thee endow."

A shiver went through her and she couldn't have

looked away from him if she wanted to. It hadn't occurred to her to wonder about their wedding night before that moment, but now she could think of little else.

Her thoughts raced as the rest of the service proceeded and she had to concentrate to keep track of what the bishop was saying. Too soon, he was leading them to sign the register. It occurred to her as she signed her name that she had no idea what Brantford's given name was. Catherine and the stranger signed as their witnesses, and then the bishop was congratulating them and handing her a copy of the marriage lines. She looked down at the paper, frowning when she realized Brantford had signed his name with an illegible scrawl that was impossible to decipher.

She had to hold in the small bubble of laughter that threatened to burst forth at the absurdity of her current situation. She didn't even know her husband's name.

CHAPTER 12

*B*RANTFORD WANTED TO ASK ROSE what she was thinking as, together, they exited the chapel, but of course he didn't. He waited patiently as she said her goodbyes to the family that had taken her in when she most needed protection.

That task now fell on him, and it was one to which he'd committed himself in the most irrevocable manner.

He'd had a moment of doubt when Rose hesitated in repeating her vows, remembering her confession that she had feelings for someone else. He couldn't help but wonder if she was mourning the loss of that love.

He hoped never to learn the name of the man who had captured her affection, for in that moment Brantford couldn't say what he would do to him. As long as Rose didn't betray her marriage vows, he would forget that his bride had hoped to wed someone else.

The carriage ride to his town house was short, and Ellen's presence helped to relieve some of the tension that now existed between him and Rose. He hadn't even had to ask for his sister's assistance. She'd simply entered the carriage after them and proceeded to engage Rose in conversation. He sat back and watched the pair, relieved when his new wife's demeanor shifted from one of cautious wariness to comfortable companionship. Perhaps one day she would learn to be relaxed when it was just the two of them.

His thoughts went to the night ahead, but he pushed them aside. Despite what everyone might think, he wasn't made of stone. He wouldn't be able to continue acting as though his emotions weren't in turmoil if he started thinking about all the things he wanted to do with Rose.

His gaze shifted to the window when they pulled up in front of his house. He'd barely had the opportunity to step down from the carriage and help his wife and sister down when the front door sprang open. He nodded to his butler, knowing that the man had arranged to have the staff line up along the front hall to greet their new mistress.

He offered Rose his arm, and she took it with a strained smile. He imagined she was more than a little overwhelmed at that moment. She'd only learned they were to be wed yesterday, and she was already entering his home as Lady Brantford.

Despite being acutely aware of Rose's presence at his side, he vowed that he'd keep his distance and give her the time she needed to adjust to her new position and to him. Ellen's presence would help to an extent.

She would no longer be acting as Rose's maid. That fiction had only been necessary while Rose stayed with Lord and Lady Overlea. Hopefully Ellen wouldn't realize he had no intention of bedding his wife right away. There were some things one didn't need to share with their sibling.

"This is Miller," Brantford said when they entered his home, introducing her to his efficient butler. "And Mrs. Warwick, the housekeeper."

Rose murmured a few words in greeting as the two bowed and curtsied to her. Mrs. Warwick introduced the rest of the staff, but he knew it would take some time for Rose to become acquainted with them all. Although Ellen had mentioned that she seemed to know many of the servants at the Overlea town house by name, and she hadn't been with them long.

Mrs. Warwick turned to Rose when she was done with the introductions and had dismissed the staff. "I'll show you to your bedroom now, my lady. Lucy will be your new maid, and she will follow."

"Thank you," Rose said.

"I'm afraid there wasn't time to arrange for a wedding breakfast," Brantford said, only then realizing that perhaps Rose had wanted one, even if the party would only have included the small group who had accompanied them to the chapel.

The smile Rose gave him held more than a hint of sadness. "I didn't expect one," she said before turning and following the housekeeper to her bedroom.

Given the haste of the entire affair, Rose might not

have expected a wedding breakfast, but he wished now that he'd thought of it.

"She'll be fine," Ellen said.

His sister's interruption startled Brantford from his musings. He hadn't even realized she was still in the hallway, hovering behind him. "I know this is very hard on her."

"Yes, but if there's one thing I've learned over the past few days it's that your new wife is very resilient. But still, her whole world has changed, and so quickly. I'm sure she just needs some time to adjust."

Brantford frowned. "I'm hardly going to storm upstairs and demand my marital rights. I understand that Rose is feeling very vulnerable right now."

Ellen tilted her head in that way she had when she was trying to divine someone's thoughts. It had always made Brantford feel a little uncomfortable when he was younger, and it still had the power to unnerve him at times.

"You've hidden him away, but I remember the sensitive youth you used to be. I'm hoping that perhaps Rose will coax him out again."

Brantford pulled an exaggerated face. "Perish the thought."

Ellen laughed. "Only time will tell, brother dear."

Brantford watched as his sister walked away. He didn't know what miracle she wanted Rose to perform, but he doubted very much that one would be forthcoming. The youth that Ellen seemed to miss was long since dead, something for which he was eternally grateful.

SHE WAS CAST ADRIFT with nothing to anchor her in place. The same thing had happened when her father had confessed to treason and turned their world upside down. She'd had her friendship with Catherine then, whose family had accepted her into their home when she hadn't wanted to leave London with her mother. She'd also come to consider Lord Kerrick a friend.

But now she was alone in Lord Brantford's town house. She hadn't thought to ask if Ellen would be staying with them. In her guise as Mrs. Blackwell, she was a widow. If that was true for Ellen as well, it was possible she had her own home.

She'd known Ellen wouldn't be pretending to be her maid forever, but at least Brantford's sister knew what was happening and Rose could speak freely to her. The same wasn't true of her new maid, a young woman who, unless Rose was mistaken, was scarce older than her own eighteen years.

And then there was Brantford.

It didn't seem real that they were married. She stared at the copy of the marriage lines the bishop had given her for a full minute, trying to convince herself she hadn't dreamed the events of that morning, while her new maid bustled about her room.

Given the reason behind their need to wed, she had no idea what to expect from her new husband. During the season, he'd never shown any indication that he'd noticed her, much as she'd wanted him to. It had taken a family scandal before he'd even had occasion to glance her way.

They were married now, but how would they proceed? It wasn't outside the realm of possibility that theirs would be a normal union. Brantford was an earl, after all. He needed to continue the family line. He wouldn't have wasted his only opportunity to secure an heir on someone he planned to keep locked up safe, but separate from him.

Much as she wanted to avoid the awkwardness of such a conversation, she needed to speak to him.

She didn't bother changing her dress. After depositing the paper that proved she was married on her dressing table, she left the maid to unpack her trunk and went in search of her husband. She wasn't surprised to find him in his study, an alarming amount of paper spread about him.

It appeared her new husband hadn't had any difficulty at all in putting her from his mind and continuing with his normal activities. A spark of annoyance flared within her.

He'd looked up from his reading when she entered the room. "Was there something you needed?" he asked, rising from his chair.

"Yes. I need to speak to you."

He lifted one brow, throwing a glance down at the papers strewn about his desk before meeting her gaze again. "Can this wait?"

"No."

He stared at her for several seconds, his expression

impassive. The man who'd shown a hint of sympathy for her was nowhere in sight. With a casual wave of his arm, he indicated she should be seated.

"Not here," Rose said, holding on to her temper, "where your attentions are clearly divided."

"No one has ever accused me of being distracted before. And I can assure you, it is not one of my failings. When I choose to speak to someone, they have my full attention."

The way he was looking at her, the weight of his gaze boring through her, left her in no doubt about that fact. It seemed as though he could see straight through to her soul.

"Very well," she said, taking the seat he'd indicated. There was no point in starting this discussion with an argument. It was already difficult enough.

He lowered himself into his seat and rested his hands on the arms of his chair, his gaze unwavering. "You needed to speak to me?"

Rose let out a soft sigh. "I know that nothing ever bothers you, but I find it more than a little uncomfortable having this conversation with you."

"We don't have to do this now. Take some time. Things have been changing at a rapid pace for you. I imagine your emotions are in turmoil."

The corners of Rose's lips lifted in a semblance of a smile she was far from feeling. "What are your feelings on… what's been happening?" She cringed slightly, hating how cowardly the question sounded. "What are your thoughts on our marriage?"

He didn't move a muscle, nor did he answer, leaving Rose to guess what he was thinking.

"Surely you'll agree that we need to discuss this."

"Not necessarily. You needed someone to protect you, and I am well suited to that task. We get along well together. Many marriages have been based on much less."

This time Rose couldn't bring herself to feign cordiality. "That is all?"

He raised that infernal brow again. "What more did you expect?"

She rose, but before she could begin to pace, she glared at Brantford. "Do not stand. The next forty or so years are going to be insufferable if you continue to treat me with polite indifference."

He hesitated, then relaxed back into his seat. "You don't wish me to treat you with respect?"

"Ugh," she said, moving toward the door to leave. She changed her mind and returned, but she didn't sit. Instead, she placed her hands on the desk and leaned forward, glaring at the smooth, unruffled stranger across the paperwork that littered its surface. "You are intolerable. Has anyone ever told you that?"

"I believe it may have come up once or twice." His mouth twitched briefly, then smoothed back into place.

She pointed a finger at him. "That was a smile."

"I have no idea what you're talking about."

"I've seen you smile before now, although I'll admit it's a rare occurrence, but always when you're trying to reassure me. But that was a smile of amusement in response to something I said."

"You're mistaken."

They stared at one another for several seconds before Rose blushed and looked away, suddenly doubting herself. No, she told herself, straightening to her full height and meeting Brantford's gaze again. She wouldn't start second-guessing herself now. There was something between them —there had to be. Brantford wouldn't have married her if she was just some woman who needed protection. The fact that he'd done so must speak to his feelings, or to the fact that he at least thought they had a chance to have a successful marriage. She had to believe that.

It was still to be determined what kind of marriage that would be.

"Will I see you later?"

"I'd planned to join you for dinner, yes. If you're bored before that, I'm sure Mrs. Warwick would be happy to give you a tour of the house. And I believe Ellen is around somewhere. Unfortunately, I have my hands full here."

She inclined her head. "Of course, my lord. And… after that?"

"After what?"

She forced herself to press on. "After dinner. Should I expect you tonight? We are newly wed, after all."

He broke his gaze briefly, but in that moment, she noticed the way his jaw flexed. Her question had surprised him.

"I think you've had enough to deal with recently."

Rose nodded. "For now? Or forever?"

"Let us get to know one another first."

Rose nodded again, content that he hadn't denied theirs would be a real marriage. Without another word, she left Brantford to his work.

CHAPTER 13

ROSE WASN'T SURE she'd be able to fall asleep that night, but after getting so little rest the night before, she settled into a dreamless sleep almost as soon as she retired.

When she woke, it took her several moments to remember where she was. She considered turning over and going back to sleep, but the morning sun was already streaming through her window. She was married now—to Brantford, impossible as that still was to believe—and she needed to begin as she meant to proceed. She wouldn't hide. In fact, she hoped they would grow closer. Certainly close enough that they'd become husband and wife in more than just name.

Pushing aside her disappointment that Brantford had coolly taken his leave of her after dinner the evening before while murmuring something about having more reports to look through, she threw off her blankets and summoned her maid. She'd already forgotten the girl's name, something for which she chided herself. She was normally very good with names, but she hadn't been herself the previous day. She needed to take control of her wandering thoughts since engaging in woolgathering wasn't going to accomplish anything.

When she finally entered the breakfast room half an hour later, she was happy to see Ellen there. She'd been too distracted the day before by thoughts of her upcoming wedding to speak to Ellen properly when she'd helped Rose to dress, and she took the opportunity to remedy that oversight.

"You look incredible," Rose said, rushing to the other woman and taking a seat next to her at the table. Her eyes roamed over Ellen's face. "I still can't believe how skilled you are with makeup. If I hadn't expected it yesterday morning, I wouldn't have recognized you. You scarce look older than I."

Ellen laughed, tiny lines crinkling at the corners of her eyes, betraying her true age. "You flatter me unduly. I think it is just the shock. I assure you, I am most definitely your senior."

"Why didn't you join us for dinner last night? I was afraid you were going to disappear on me and I'd never see you again."

Ellen looked at her intently, and heat began to rise in her cheeks. Which was silly, really, because there was nothing for her to be embarrassed about. Unfortunately.

"I thought you and my brother needed some time alone together."

Rose stood then, going to the sideboard to take a plate. Her gaze moved over the alarming amount of food, but she took only some scrambled eggs and a slice of toast. Until her nerves settled, she wasn't sure she'd be able to keep down more than that.

"Speaking of my new husband, where is he?" she asked when she returned to the table.

"He's already eaten and has gone out. Said he had a few meetings to attend."

Of course he did, Rose thought, trying to hold back her disappointment. "I'm sure he's a very busy man. I remember whenever I spotted him at a ball or event, he had almost as many admirers as I! Both men and women. They seemed to surround him like bees to honey."

Ellen smiled around the sip of tea she was taking. "You noticed him, did you?"

Rose laughed. "Of course I did. Everyone does. For all the good it did me. It was clear he didn't want anything to do with the people who claimed his attention, and I think because of that they sought it all the more."

"You're very astute," Ellen said. "That's how he operates. He sets himself apart, acting as though he doesn't care at all for anyone or anything that is happening around him, and so everyone jumps to seek his favor." Ellen shook her head. "I don't know how he does it, actually. I've tried mimicking that behavior and it earned me nothing. I became invisible."

"I doubt that very much," Rose said. "Unless you

are trying to look older and matronly, I'm sure you attract attention everywhere you go."

Ellen laughed. "Have I mentioned how much I like you? You're very good for the ego."

Rose figured now was as good a time as any to try to glean a little additional information. "Would you care to answer a few questions for me?"

Ellen let out a soft breath. "I figured you'd want answers. Just let me fortify myself," she said, taking another sip of tea. When she was done, she placed her hands in her lap and faced Rose fully. "I'll answer what questions I can. But I'm afraid that if you want details concerning my brother, you'll have to ask him."

Rose frowned. "No, actually. I wanted to know more about you. I know nothing except that your name is Ellen Blackwell, and I don't even know if that is your real name. Or if you're married."

Ellen looked away for a moment. "That is my name, technically. It's actually Lady Laughton. Blackwell was Lord Laughton's family name."

Rose racked her brain, trying to remember whether she'd met Ellen's husband. "I don't recall meeting Lord Laughton. How does he feel about your posing as a maid?"

"You wouldn't have met him. I'm now the Dowager Viscountess Laughton. The new viscount doesn't like balls and tends to act the hermit."

"Oh, I'm so sorry," Rose said. "If it would help, I'm here if you ever need to talk about it or about what happened. I'm hardly in a position to spread gossip, not that I ever did before my family was ruined."

Ellen looked away again. "Maybe one day I will. It's no secret that my husband was killed in a hunting accident two years ago. To fill my time since his passing, I occasionally help my brother when he needs someone to get close to another woman." Ellen shrugged and turned to face her again. "My brother does it to keep me out of trouble."

Rose's interest was sparked by that cryptic comment. "Now I'm dying to know all the details."

"Yes, I imagine you are. But right now that's all I'm going to share."

"I understand," Rose said, turning back to her breakfast and finishing her toast. She looked at her eggs but didn't think she could eat them after all.

"I know you have a lot on your mind," Ellen said. "Other than divulging all my darkest secrets—which, if we're both being truthful, you'll no doubt discover sooner rather than later—I wish I knew what to say to ease your mind."

Rose gave her a sidelong glance before taking a sip of her own tea. "Just having you here is helping me tremendously. And I assume I can ask Catherine to visit from time to time?"

"Of course. She's more than welcome here. This is your home now. You don't need to ask my permission for anything."

"But I should ask Brantford?"

Ellen scrunched her nose. "Not for everything, no.

I'm sure it will be an adjustment for him having you here. It's been a few years since I lived here, after all, but he won't begrudge you your friends."

Ellen's eyes narrowed, and Rose got the distinct impression that her new sister-in-law was holding something back.

"You may as well tell me now," Rose said.

Ellen shook her head. "It amazes me how observant you are for one so young."

Rose bristled a little at that comment but said nothing since it wasn't untrue. She'd come out that year, but she couldn't help but feel that perhaps she was a little too young for her husband. She wasn't sure how old he was, but he had to be at least thirty. She wondered how much older Ellen was than her brother.

"My brother can be a difficult man to get to know, so I'm going to stick my nose in where it doesn't belong right now," Ellen said, interrupting her thoughts.

Rose waved her hand. "You might as well. I could use some advice when it comes to my husband."

"Brantford has always felt as though he had to prove himself. Father was very difficult on him. On both of us, really. Our parents weren't exactly the type to show affection, but they were harder on him since he was the heir."

Rose didn't say anything, but it wasn't as though such an upbringing was uncommon.

"My brother has an unidentifiable quality, a type of charisma that draws people to him. But—and if you tell him I told you this, I'll deny it to my dying breath—he's always been shy. He hated the way people hovered around him when, most of the time, he just wanted to be left alone."

"Really? Brantford is shy?"

"Perhaps not anymore," Ellen said with a shrug, "but he definitely was as a child and a youth. He's learned to turn that around though and to use his charisma to his own advantage. People *want* to please him, and it's amazing what they will do to gain his approval."

Rose frowned as a horrible thought occurred to her. It would certainly explain why her husband hadn't come to her the previous night though. She wasn't sure she wanted to know the answer to her question.

She took a deep breath and asked, "Does Brantford have a mistress?"

Ellen looked surprised at the question. "No… I mean, I don't know for sure, but I don't think so."

"What makes you say that?"

"It's not as though he'd ever discuss such a thing with me, so I can only guess. But I don't think he'd have such a long-standing arrangement with one woman."

"He married me, which I'm sure came as a shock to you. To myself as well. It's possible you don't know him as well as you think." The thought depressed her.

Ellen tilted her head and considered her statement. "My brother loves his secrets, and he's always going out to meet people at odd hours of the day and night. I'm sure he's had liaisons, but a mistress that he's set up and sees on a regular basis? I very much doubt it."

Rose looked away, not wanting to discuss the matter further. She hoped that Ellen was correct, but how much would the other woman know about her brother's private life?

"You can't give up on him, Rose."

Ellen's statement brought her out of her reverie, and she turned to meet the older woman's gaze.

"Let me guess, you haven't consummated your marriage yet."

If she were able, Rose would disappear through the floor. The sympathy on Ellen's face was almost too much to bear.

"I'm not sure how it happened, but you're different. My brother cares for you. He wouldn't have married you if he didn't."

"He wanted to keep me safe—"

"I can't even count the number of times he's asked me to get close to a woman to gain information for him, or to aid in keeping her safe if she was in danger. And there have been at least two occasions where those women almost died from the threats they faced. But you're the only one he allowed to get this close."

Rose shook her head. "I want to believe that, but... I don't know what to do. How can I find out when he's keeping me at a distance?"

"He feels guilty, I'm sure. Feels as though he'd be taking advantage of you."

"That's absurd."

"Not if he told you he was marrying you to keep you

safe. I assume, during that conversation, he said nothing to you about his feelings."

"No. I assumed he was being practical about my situation. I'd hoped though that I could make him care, but I can't do that if he won't allow me to get close to him."

Ellen reached out to squeeze her hand. "You have to be relentless. He's trying to be noble, but if you want this marriage to be a real one, you'll have to make him see just how much you want it."

Rose closed her eyes briefly. "This has the potential to be humiliating."

"Yes, but it also has the potential to be wonderful. My brother deserves happiness, as do you. I know that you care for him, and it's obvious to me that he cares for you. You just have to make him realize it."

Rose considered the other woman's words as Ellen rose and excused herself. She'd played the coquette all season, but somehow it felt different doing so with Brantford. What if he pushed her away? She wasn't sure she'd survive the humiliation. But what if Ellen was correct and he didn't?

CHAPTER 14

BRANTFORD HADN'T SEEN ROSE since dinner the evening before, but he was acutely aware of her presence in his home. He wasn't running away exactly when he left after breaking his fast since he did have people he needed to see. But he'd seized upon the opportunity to give himself space.

Dinner had been an awkward affair. He'd behaved as though they were polite acquaintances, not wanting to put any undue pressure on Rose. She'd hardly had any choice in the matter of their marriage, after all. But they'd fallen into silences that were more than a little awkward. He'd hoped Rose's outgoing nature would help to ease those tense moments. From what he'd witnessed of her behavior toward others, she was far from shy. The fact that she hadn't been comfortable at all told him he needed to make more of an effort.

He wasn't used to being the one courting another's favor. He'd lived his whole life with others seeking his approval, and the more reticent he was in giving it, the more they sought it. For some reason, that wasn't working with Rose.

He wondered, for what seemed like the millionth time, whom Rose had hoped to wed in his stead. Somehow after this whole ordeal with Standish and her father was done, he'd have to go about the business of wooing his own wife.

It was early evening when he finally returned home, and he wondered if Rose had already eaten.

Miller was waiting for him and gave him a meaningful look before leading Brantford to the study. The fact that the man wanted privacy for this conversation had all his senses on high alert. Something was wrong, and his butler didn't want his new mistress to overhear them.

"What happened?" Brantford asked when Miller closed the study door behind them.

"A package arrived for Lady Brantford."

He didn't swear but he wanted to. He looked at his desk and saw the package in question resting on its surface. "Do you know who sent it?"

"I'm afraid there was no return address. It was left on the doorstep. I don't know how long it was there before it was discovered."

Brantford approached the package, which was wrapped in nondescript brown paper, simple twine holding the whole thing together. His jaw clenched when he saw it was addressed to "Miss Rose Hardwick."

Since the package was delivered to his doorstep, the sender would have known she was now his wife.

He had no doubt that Standish was trying to provoke a reaction out of him. He would know that Brantford wouldn't allow his wife to open a mysterious delivery.

"Has Lady Brantford seen this?"

"No. I made sure to keep it from her."

"Good." Brantford reached for a slim knife he kept in his top desk drawer and cut through the twine. The paper fell away to reveal a plain white box. He lifted the top to find another box inside.

Annoyance flared. He hated the games played by men who were trying far too hard to be clever and mysterious. He could just imagine the glee on Standish's face as he put together the package and half expected that, in the end, it would contain nothing.

Not willing to take that chance, however, he opened that box and the smaller one within. Finally, inside the third box, he found a folded, unsealed piece of paper. He opened it where it lay within the box, his heart stuttering when it revealed a strand of chestnut-colored hair.

"Where is Lady Brantford?" His voice was sharper than normal, but under the circumstances he could hardly be expected to maintain his usual aplomb.

"She is upstairs in her bedroom." Miller didn't ask what was in the package—he'd wait for Brantford to volunteer that information if it was necessary. But he was clearly taken aback by the urgency in his master's voice.

"Close that all up and lock it away," Brantford said, striding to the door without a backward glance.

He took the stairs two at a time, his heart racing. It wasn't Rose's hair. It couldn't be. If he wasn't mistaken, the shade was too red to belong to his wife. Still, if Standish had been hoping to provoke a reaction, he'd succeeded. Brantford needed to see for himself that Rose was safe.

ROSE WAS IN THE MIDDLE OF WRITING A LETTER to her mother when her bedroom door swung open. Surprised, she smeared the ink.

Sighing, she set aside her lap desk and turned to see who would enter what she'd hoped would be her private domain without so much as a knock. The last person she expected to see standing in the doorway was her husband.

There was a wild look in his eyes that filled her with dread. Before she could speak, Brantford strode into the room.

"Stand up, please," he said.

Something was most definitely wrong. "What has happened?" she asked, rising to face him. "My father…?" She was afraid to ask the question. They wouldn't have hung him already, would they? Surely

Brantford would have told her and allowed her to see him first.

"Take down your hair."

"You're scaring me, Brantford."

He ignored her, and when she didn't move to do as he'd asked, he shifted so he stood behind her and began to unpin her hair himself. She remained silent while he worked. When he was finished, he spread her tresses between his hands. She looked over her shoulder and caught him examining a strand.

"Please tell me why you're acting this way."

Brantford met her gaze, then looked away. In that moment, his relief was unmistakable. "Standish is playing games. He wanted me to think he'd harmed you in some way."

She turned to face him. "You were afraid."

He met her gaze. "Yes."

They stayed like that for several seconds, then with a nod in her direction, he turned to leave.

"Wait!" It came out a little louder than she'd expected, but in the short time he'd been in her room, she'd come to wonder if Ellen was correct about her brother caring for her. And it was clear to her that he fully intended to leave her alone, again.

"I'm sorry that I frightened you, but I had to see for myself that you were safe."

"I am." She stepped closer, then took a deep breath and, before she lost her nerve, said, "You don't have to leave."

His expression shuttered, and her confidence faltered. Despite that, she pressed on. "We're married. You don't have to be so careful around me. When I agreed to become your wife, I expected to become one in every way."

He frowned. "If you think to play me like you did those who surrounded you so eagerly all year, you should know that I am not so easily led."

She licked her lips, and a shiver of awareness swept through her when he followed the movement. "I'd be perfectly content to allow you to take the lead."

His eyes darkened, and she found herself holding her breath.

"You have no idea what you're proposing."

She dared to take another step toward him and placed a hand on his arm. "What makes you think I'm innocent?"

It was a lie, of course, and she was fairly certain he knew it. Still, it was possible Brantford would take her at her word. Instead, he took a step back and she let her hand fall to her side.

Torn between grief and anger, she didn't bother to hold back her thoughts. "I was beginning to think you had a modicum of feeling buried somewhere beneath that ice-cold facade of yours. But it's true what everyone says. You have ice water running through your veins."

Despite the fact they were in her bedroom, she turned and started for the door, needing to get away from him. She only managed two steps before he reached out and grabbed her hand, halting her progress. For a moment she was torn, conscious of the heat of his hand engulfing hers. Her pride urged her to tug her hand from his grasp and leave the room, but her traitorous heart hoped he'd changed his mind.

Her heart won and she turned to face him. Her pride wouldn't allow her to throw herself at him again, however.

"You've made it abundantly clear that ours will be a marriage in name only."

In reply, he tugged her closer. Mere inches separated them, and she waited, hoping he'd pull her even closer but expecting him to drop her hand and walk away from her.

CHAPTER 15

*H*E SHOULD HAVE ALLOWED HER TO DEPART. He'd reached out to her without conscious thought, and now that she was so close, he ached to pull her against him. If she were anyone else, he wouldn't be having this struggle.

But he couldn't let her go.

"Would that I were made of ice. Then nothing you say or do would affect me."

He knew that admitting his weakness when it came to his wife would give her power over him. Power he normally yielded to no one.

The moment that followed stretched between them, heavy with awareness. The only sound in the room was that of his breathing, which sounded unnaturally loud to his own ears. He told himself to release her hand and loosened his grip. He saw the realization in her eyes that he was going to turn her away. Again. Saw the hint of defeat reflected there before she could hide it. That, more than any plea she could have made, had him lowering his head.

He'd just have a taste of her, then he'd do what needed to be done.

But when she made a soft sound of contented surprise, one that sounded like surrender, and raised her arms to rest her hands on his shoulders, he knew he was lost. He grabbed her by the hips and pulled her against his body.

What started as a simple pressing of his lips against hers deepened until he was all but ravaging her mouth, plundering within its depths much as he longed to surge within her body. He would have pulled away then, calling himself all sorts of names for treating Rose in such a manner, but she buried her hands in his hair and nipped at his departing lips.

"Don't you dare stop now," she said as she resumed their kiss.

His much-touted control was cast aside without a care as he molded her body against his. He might have growled, so great was his need, but instead of inciting fear in her, Rose responded with a breathy moan that had his hardening cock twitching in anticipation of what was to come.

There was no stopping now, and in that moment he didn't care.

His entire world centered on the woman in his arms. She fit against him perfectly, just as he'd always known she would. She also was no shy maiden, although he didn't believe her prevarication earlier about her innocence. But his new wife had a natural sensuality to her that drew every male eye. That he would be the first to initiate her into the world of passion was more than he'd ever expected. Certainly it was more than he deserved.

Yet here she was, and he was tired of pushing her away. Tonight he would concentrate only on the woman in his arms.

Her hands were under his coat, nimble fingers undoing the buttons of his waistcoat. He wanted to tell her to slow down, but her sense of urgency sparked a similar desperation within him. If they stopped or held back, this moment might not end where they both needed it to.

And so instead of stilling her movements, he ran his hands along the hooks that marched down the back of her dress. It didn't take him long, and he was pulling apart the fabric just as she spread his waistcoat open and splayed her hands across his abdomen.

He groaned then, the feel of her hands, which were resting just above his trousers, causing a temporary madness to take hold. He spared only a moment to wonder at just what it was about this woman that could cause him to lose control so quickly. Many others had tried—he was no monk, certainly—but he'd always maintained his distance even while he spent himself inside their bodies. But with Rose...

His thoughts shattered when she lowered a hand to cover his hardness through his trousers, and he tore his mouth from hers.

"You are the very devil," he said, his voice barely above a croak.

"If that's what you need to believe to tempt you to sin, then I willingly agree."

With that she took a step away from him and allowed her dress to fall to the floor. "Would you prefer to watch or take a more active role?"

Her fingers toyed with the edge of her chemise and his mind went blank. All thoughts of others no longer had any place here. There was only a delightfully sensuous Rose and himself. And right then he wasn't content to simply stand back and watch. He was all in now, and he would be the one divesting her of her clothing.

She dropped her hand and watched him as he set about unlacing the corset she wore. When he freed the garment and tossed it aside, a kind of madness overtook him and he swept her chemise up and over her head, desperate to bare the rest of her body.

He didn't touch her yet, his restraint costing him more than he would have thought possible. But remembering her earlier words, he realized that he was content to step back and watch this last part.

Rose was naked now save for her stockings.

"Remove them," he said, his eyes roving over her body. He was surprised that his voice was steady as he issued the command. His emotions were anything but. He wanted to rip the stockings from her body, but a small shred of sanity had returned, reminding him that despite her bravado, Rose was still a maiden. He wanted her to remember this night forever, and he didn't want those memories to be of him savagely taking her without a thought for her pleasure.

He almost swallowed his tongue when she bent down to do as he commanded, realizing that he had erred. He should have just left the damned stockings on. The sight of her bending before him, her tongue sweeping across that plump lower lip, had him stifling a groan.

He must have made a sound, however, because Rose glanced up at him. He caught the uncertainty in her expression before she masked it, and he realized she was more nervous than she wanted him to believe. Their gazes met and held for several seconds before she looked away and resumed her task with quick, efficient movements. Another time he'd have her repeat this action more slowly, but right now he was anxious to move to the bed.

He'd just shrugged out of his coat and waistcoat, not bothering to fold them meticulously as he normally did, and tossed them onto a chair in a casual heap when she straightened.

Rose was perfect, softly rounded in all the right places, her hair framing her face and breasts in a rich waterfall of color.

"Are you going to disrobe?" The quiver in her voice was faint but unmistakable. He knew that a great deal of it stemmed from the heat flowing between them, but there was a hint of fear beneath it. No, not fear. She wanted this as much as he did. But it would be her first time, and what woman wouldn't be thinking about the pain that was about to come?

He reached for her then, tugging her into his arms, and she came willingly. She raised her head as he lowered his, their mouths meeting in an almost violent clash.

He explored her then, one hand reaching down to stroke, then cup her breast while the other grasped her hip and dragged her firmly against him. When he shifted that hand lower and dragged her leg up around his hip so he could press his hardness against her core, her moan tore through him like wildfire.

This time it was almost impossible to step back.

"On the bed," he said, another thrill of anticipation shooting through him as she hurried to comply. He made quick work of the rest of his clothing, aware that she was watching his every move. When he straightened again after removing his trousers and smallclothes, Rose didn't hide her gasp.

He was large, yes, but she'd have no basis for comparison. At least he hoped very much that was the case. It had never mattered to him before how many lovers his previous bedmates had had, but suddenly it was vitally important to him that he be Rose's first.

He shook away that thought and lowered himself onto the bed beside her, reaching out to bring her to him. The shock of her flesh against his was sweet madness.

"Don't be afraid," he said, staring into her beautiful blue eyes, willing her to hear what he'd left unsaid. That he would be careful, that he would make sure she enjoyed their coming together.

He started his exploration with a kiss, but it wasn't long before he was dragging his mouth down the side of her throat and across her breast, taking a nipple into his mouth. He couldn't stop looking up at her face, trying to gauge her responses. He'd stop if she gave any indication she'd changed her mind, but he didn't expect that to happen. He was actually watching for her confirmation that she was enjoying this as much as he was.

When she threaded her fingers through his hair, he switched and gave her other breast attention, his hands wandering lower. He hesitated when he reached the apex of her thighs, needing her approval before continuing. She took her lip between her teeth, which elicited a groan from him, and nodded.

When he touched her core, he was relieved to find she was already wet for him.

"Is it supposed to be like this?" she asked on a low moan.

He couldn't stop the smile that spread over his face. "Only if the man actually cares about bringing pleasure to his partner."

"And you care?"

Their eyes met and held, his body frozen over hers.

"About this, yes," he said finally.

"Have…" She looked away quickly, then seemed to collect herself and faced him again. "Have I ruined things?"

He kissed her gently. "Not possible."

"Then please don't stop."

Pure, unadulterated need shot through him. "I have no intention of stopping."

He tried to go slowly, draw out every drop of joy from this moment. Tonight would be the first of many more nights together, but he would do everything in his power to make it special for her. To imprint himself on her mind and body, just as she was doing to him. Every moan, every tentative touch, only served to increase his need for her.

He used his hands and his mouth, helping her to reach her peak twice before he finally entered her. When he did, it took every ounce of willpower he possessed not to rut on her like an animal. Rose had played the vixen many times, but his instincts had proven correct. She was untouched, and he hated that he'd caused her even a moment of pain.

"I'm sorry," he murmured before kissing her again.

"No," she said, and he stilled, pulling away to look down on her. She touched his cheek, cupping it, a look of wonder on her face. "Never apologize for this."

Words failed him, and so he started moving then. She let out a breathless "oooh" of sound, dropping her hand to clutch at his shoulder. Her other hand grasped his backside, urging him to go faster.

It was over far too quickly, but at least he hadn't embarrassed himself. He'd held out until she reached her peak.

As he drifted off to sleep, a content and sleepy Rose clinging to him, he had a startling moment of clarity.

If he wasn't careful, he could find himself breaking all his carefully constructed rules for this woman by allowing her into his heart.

BLISS, PURE AND SIMPLE, SETTLED OVER ROSE. She didn't think she'd be able to move from her position even if she wanted to. She lay snuggled up against Brantford, her head on his chest while he held her. One warm hand gripped her arm, the other smoothed up and down her back.

"Brantford?"

The hand on her back stilled and Rose held her breath, wondering if her husband would pull away from her. Finally, after several seconds, he continued stroking her.

"Yes?"

She lifted her head and looked directly at him. "What is your given name?"

For a moment, she thought he wasn't going to tell her. Then, finally, he said, "Lucien."

"Lucien." She allowed the name to settle in her mind, enjoying the way it rolled off her tongue. She knew it meant light, and she realized that was what he was to her. Her light in the darkness, guiding her through the murky chaos her life had become. "I like it."

"No one calls me by it."

"Not even your sister?"

"Especially not my sister."

His vehemence surprised her. "Why not? She's older than you, and you only inherited your title after your father passed away. It would be natural for her to call you Lucien when it is just the two of you alone together."

He pressed a hand to the back of her head, guiding her back down to rest on his chest. She thought the conversation was over and was just drifting off to sleep when he said, "If you'd like, you can call me that. But only when we are alone together. I do have a reputation to maintain."

If it was possible, Rose's heart melted even further. They'd just shared the physical act of love, but this... Brantford—no, Lucien—was letting her into his heart. He didn't know it, of course, and he'd couched it in terms that said he was only humoring her. But she knew he was allowing her an intimacy that no one else shared.

"Good night, Lucien," she said, dropping a kiss on his chest before closing her eyes and drifting off to sleep.

She didn't know if the kiss she felt him place on the top of her head was real or the beginning of a pleasant dream.

CHAPTER 16

$\mathcal{R}$OSE AND ELLEN entered the breakfast room together the following morning. His sister cast a sly smile in his direction, but Brantford ignored her. Ellen had taken to trying to get a rise out of him far too often of late.

He considered his wife as the two of them moved to the sideboard to fill their plates, chattering together about the weather. He couldn't believe he'd spent the entire night in his wife's bed, something he'd never done before with any of his lovers. But then he'd seldom seen the same woman more than once, hating how clingy they could become given the slightest encouragement. It baffled him that he had no such qualms when it came to Rose.

After the closeness they'd shared, he was reluctant to bring up the subject of her father and shatter her good spirits. But reality couldn't be held at bay, and he was nothing if not practical.

"We need to speak to your mother," he said when they were seated.

Rose, who'd only glanced briefly at him when she entered the room, met his gaze. There was a newfound confidence in her that he found almost irresistible. It should bother him just how easily she'd wrapped him around her finger. It seemed he was exactly like all the other men who'd vied for her attention during the season.

"I've started writing a letter to her, but I was interrupted. I'll finish it today."

Ellen let out a small snort of laughter when Rose mentioned being interrupted, and he glanced at her sharply. Surely Rose hadn't told her what had taken place between them.

Pushing aside that uncomfortable thought, he continued. "No, I mean I need to speak to her in person about your father, and I want you to come with me. I've already sent word of our marriage, and I'm sure she'll want to see you in person."

A spark of annoyance entered Rose's expression. "I'm not going to allow you to deposit me with her while you continue looking into this matter."

Brantford took a sip of his tea before replying. "Perish the thought. I can only imagine what sort of trouble you'd get into on your own. No, I plan to keep you by my side where I can keep an eye on you."

Rose's eyes softened, and he found himself smiling at her in response. His sister's light, tinkling laugh broke into the intimate moment that had developed between them.

"Oh, you two are simply adorable. I'll make sure to have my things packed right away. When are we leaving?"

Brantford glared at Ellen. "You're not coming with us."

"But—" Rose began.

"The last thing I need is my sister watching my every move, making snide little comments about our marriage." He barely held in a small shudder at the thought. He could tell himself that Ellen didn't really know anything, but that would change if she accompanied them. After all, it wasn't as though he planned to procure separate rooms for them at the coaching inn.

Ellen leaned back in her chair, the corners of her mouth lifting in a small, self-satisfied manner. "I'm sure I can keep myself occupied in town while the two of you are away. The Duke of Castlefield is still in town, after all. And don't think I've forgiven you for not telling me he'd be at your wedding."

"Leave the poor man alone, Ellen. Haven't you already done enough?"

Rose looked back and forth between them as they spoke. "Was that who you had standing with you, Lucien? Isn't he the man they call the Unsuitable Duke? There were all sorts of rumors about him, but I don't believe I saw him before our wedding."

"That's because my evil sister has all but driven him away from polite society."

Ellen crossed her arms and smiled. "I may have been the source of one or two small rumors… and I will claim credit for the name."

Rose's hands went to her mouth. "You didn't? You're the reason everyone calls him that?"

"Indeed," Brantford said, feeling more than a hint of pity for the man he considered his closest friend. He'd cultivated his own moniker of the Unaffected Earl because it suited him in his dealings, but Castlefield had been branded as the Unsuitable Duke by his sister, and it had caused him all manner of trouble. Rumors about him had sprung up seemingly overnight, and despite her protests to the contrary, he knew Ellen had a hand in most of them.

"Which rumors are true? Some of them seem to contradict each other, and I confess I'm more than a little curious."

"No," Brantford said, glaring at his sister. "You will not bring my wife into your machinations against the Duke. You're bad enough on your own. Don't you think it's time you left him in peace?"

Ellen lifted a shoulder, but her expression didn't change. "I won't do anything to him. Well, nothing that would cause him irreparable harm."

He could tell Rose was eager to ask Ellen for all the details. "I thought you didn't engage in gossip."

"Is it gossip if I'm speaking to the source? Surely Ellen has a reason for her actions."

"It doesn't matter. We're going to be leaving tomorrow, and I thought I'd take you to visit your father later today."

Rose was instantly diverted from discussing his sister's schemes, but that wasn't the reason he'd made the offer. The smile on her face was all the reward he needed.

"I thought I wasn't allowed to see him again."

"Not without me, no. But given the circumstances, I don't think there would be any harm." What he didn't say was that he'd already put her in increased danger when they'd visited her father together. But as long as he remained by her side, she would be safe. He'd see to it.

CHAPTER 17

THEIR CARRIAGE SET OUT EARLY the next morning, rumbling along the streets of London. Rose tried not to worry about the reason for the outriders that accompanied them. Brantford had said he would keep her safe, and she trusted him.

The first night they'd spent together had been more than she could have dreamed of. She'd thought that perhaps it signaled a change in their relationship, but Brantford hadn't come to her last night. If she had to provoke him to get him to pay her any kind of attention, she'd oblige. For now. But she knew it would get tiresome very quickly.

Was her husband capable of change? He'd settled back into the remote person she'd always known after their breakfast yesterday morning. At the moment, he sat opposite her in the carriage, buried behind the *Times*. Several more newspapers lay stacked on the seat next to him. At least he hadn't brought any reports with him.

"Lucien?"

Brantford peered over the top of the paper. His eyes narrowed, and she knew he was trying to divine what she was planning to ask him.

"I have a question."

He folded the broadsheet and placed it on top of the other papers. "I'd assumed as much. You don't need to preface it."

She wrinkled her nose. "Very funny. I was trying to get your attention first."

"You have it."

His gaze drifted down to the neckline of her dress and heat went through her. Was he remembering the night they'd consummated their marriage? She'd been unable to think of little else.

"Do you think the carriage driver can hear our discussion?"

Her husband raised a brow. "Over the sound of the wheels on the cobblestones? I doubt it. Why?"

She leaned forward and licked her lips. Brantford's gaze moved from her eyes to her décolletage again before returning to her face. Rose barely contained a smile of satisfaction.

"This past spring, I heard a rumor."

His brows drew together. "I won't indulge in tormenting Castlefield. My sister has done enough."

"No," she said, shaking her head. "Not those. I know I'll need to speak to Ellen directly to learn why she dislikes His Grace so much."

"Rose…" He didn't have to voice the rest of his admonishment.

"This was an entirely unrelated tale."

He let out a breath, which she took as a sign that she was breaking through his reserved detachment.

"Go ahead and ask, but I can't guarantee I'll have any answers for you."

She frowned. He hadn't denied that he'd know about the rumor in question, just that he might not be able to give her any more information. She knew Brantford was full of secrets, but she was fairly certain she'd be able to draw this one out of him.

"I won't share any names because I know what it's like to have people whispering about you. Even when the gossip is true, it still causes pain."

He raised a brow and waited.

"It's just that, well…" She swallowed and forced herself to continue. It was silly to be shy discussing this with her husband given what they had already shared. "There was a rumor about a certain lord and lady engaging in… intimate relations." When Brantford didn't reply, she continued. "In a carriage."

His brow lowered and he remained silent for several seconds. When he finally spoke, he was his normal composed self. "What is it you wish to know? If it's true? That would be hard to confirm without the names of the individuals in question."

She shook her head again. "I don't care if it's true. I was just wondering if it was *possible*. I mean, in a carriage!"

Brantford's lips curled up in amusement, a glint in his eyes causing Rose's heart to skip a beat. "It's definitely possible."

She released a slow breath. An inexplicable shyness had her hesitating before she shored up her courage. "It is? Do you think… Could you show me?"

The heat that entered Brantford's eyes at her request had her feeling like a wanton. But who was she fooling? When it came to her husband, one night had been enough to show her that she craved his touch.

Disappointment flooded through her when he turned to the window, but it was short-lived when she saw him draw the curtain. She hastened to do the same for the other window before turning to face him. He'd settled back on the bench opposite her, his eyes intent as he stared at her.

"I'd planned to give you time to adjust to the physical side of marriage."

"Which is why you didn't join me last night."

"Just so," he said with a slight inclination of his head. "I never imagined you'd be quite so… curious."

She licked her lips again, confidence surging through her when Brantford followed the movement. She knew he wouldn't welcome an excess of emotion, but she did want him to know how wrong he was in his assumptions. "I was disappointed when I didn't see you."

He continued to watch her, his normally pale eyes dark in the dim light of the carriage. She waited, knowing her patience would be rewarded. Brantford wouldn't have closed the curtains if he meant to deny her curiosity.

After what felt like an eternity, he rose and moved to sit next to her on the bench. She shifted to look at him, desire clogging her throat at the intent way he stared at her. It was so unlike his normal demeanor, but she'd already seen this side of him when they'd consummated their marriage.

"Lucien—"

He lowered his head, cutting off whatever she was going to say when he took her mouth in a passionate kiss. Rose made an eager noise as she leaned closer and settled into his embrace. She felt the muscles shift in his arms, and her world tilted sideways before she realized his intent. She found herself seated sideways across his lap.

He leaned back and looked down at her, his eyes almost black now. "You, Lady Brantford, are dangerous."

A shiver of delight coursed through her at the way he looked at her as though he wanted to consume her whole.

"I could say the same thing about you."

A corner of his mouth lifted. "Indeed," he said before lowering his head again to claim her mouth.

She was enjoying the way he seemed intent on devouring her, moving first to clasp his shoulders, then to thread her fingers through his fair hair. She marveled at how soft it was, so at odds with the hard planes of his chest and the muscles of his arms and legs.

His hands moved up and down her back, but she didn't realize what he was doing until her bodice loosened. He pushed her dress down her shoulders and then set to work on her corset. She hadn't believed it was possible to make love in a carriage, although she'd hoped Brantford would prove her wrong. He was doing exactly that.

Anxious to feel him, she tore her mouth from his and set about unbuttoning his waistcoat. Her breathing was ragged, but so was his. He'd had a head start, and Brantford had her corset off by the time she reached the last button and started to undo his cravat. She made a small sound of distress as she fumbled with the knot, and her husband's hands reached up to cover hers.

"Leave it," he said.

Grumbling in response, she dragged her hands down his chest and abdomen, then taking fistfuls of his shirt, tugged the material from his trousers. She slid her hands underneath the fabric, caressing his heated skin. Brantford let out a harsh laugh.

"I'd thought to go slow."

"I've been waiting months for you. I think that is slow enough." She realized what she had revealed as soon as the words left her mouth. She looked away, embarrassed.

Brantford settled his hands on each side of her face and turned her to face him. "Months?"

He wouldn't let her hide, so she settled for closing her eyes.

"Look at me, Rose."

It wasn't the demand so much as the way his thumbs were stroking over her cheeks and tracing over her lips that had her opening her eyes again. His gaze was intent, and she could almost feel him reaching into the depths of her soul.

"Yes, months. I might have had a mild infatuation with you since arriving in London at the start of the season."

His fingers stilled, but he kept her face cradled in his hands. "You led me to believe you had feelings for someone else. I'd assumed our marriage was a disappointment to you."

"No, it wasn't. It was everything I'd ever dreamed of. Especially now that you are no longer keeping your distance from me."

She wanted to tell him that she loved him, but it was too soon. Her husband almost never revealed his emotions. He wouldn't welcome the idea of his wife mooning over him like a silly schoolgirl. She'd have to show him she was as sophisticated as the women with whom he no doubt consorted to satisfy his desires. For if there was one thing she'd learned, he was no novice in the art of lovemaking.

"I don't know what to say."

She smiled at him, determined not to allow her embarrassing confession to come between them. "Don't say anything. Just continue with what we were doing. I believe I was about to do this…"

She started to unbutton his trousers, but he kept her face tilted toward his. When she reached inside to stroke his hard length, he closed his eyes and lowered his head to kiss her again.

"Never let it be said," he murmured against her mouth, "that I wouldn't do everything in my power to satisfy my wife's curiosity."

Her world was upended again, and she let out a small shriek of surprise. When everything settled, she was lying on her back on the carriage bench, her husband poised over her. His grin was decidedly wicked and threatened to steal her breath.

"My curiosity knows no bounds," she said, delighting in this unexpectedly playful side of her husband.

"Well then, perhaps we should get started."

She could only moan in response as her husband went about divesting her of her clothing. She didn't even care that he'd left most of his on when he finally pushed inside her.

"Lucien…"

"Yes, Rose," he replied without slowing his movements.

Somehow she held back her confession of love. It wasn't time yet, but hopefully she'd soon be able to share her feelings with her husband. If the fates were kind, perhaps he might one day come to return them.

CHAPTER 18

*I*T WAS LATE WHEN THEY FINALLY ARRIVED at her aunt's estate in Essex. They'd changed horses at a coaching inn along the way, stopping only for a midday meal and dinner. Brantford had wanted to spend the night at the inn where they'd eaten, concerned for her comfort, but she'd insisted they press on since they were already near their destination.

But Rose did take the time to set her clothing and hair to rights before setting off for the final leg of their journey. The last thing she wanted was to see her mother again while looking disheveled. Even if her mother didn't guess what she and Brantford had been doing in the carriage—two times, no less!—Mama would worry that the stress of their current situation had caused her so much heartache that Rose had allowed herself to become run-down. The very last thing she wanted to do was to cause her mother any additional grief.

Her aunt's butler had barely had time to open the door when her mother was rushing into the entrance hall.

"I'm so happy to see you, Rose," Lady Worthington said, sweeping her into a hug. "I was so worried about your decision to remain in London."

"I am well, Mama," Rose said, worried at the dark circles under her mother's eyes. She followed her to the drawing room. "Where is Aunt Augusta?"

"She wanted to give us a few minutes alone together before welcoming you both. She knows how concerned I've been about you."

"Lord and Lady Overlea watched over me. And as you've heard, Lord Brantford has since taken over that role."

Lady Worthington dabbed at her eyes with a linen handkerchief and gave Brantford a tearful smile. "It is more than I expected, especially after your betrothal ended."

"I know you didn't approve of my actions, but I couldn't marry Lord Kerrick when he was in love with my best friend. And as you see, everything has turned out for the best." Her mother looked unconvinced, so Rose took hold of her hands and pulled her down to the settee next to her. "I am not just trying to put your mind at ease. I am happy."

Lady Worthington turned then to Brantford, who had settled into an armchair. "Words cannot express how grateful I am to you, my lord. When everyone abandoned us and when my stubborn daughter ended her betrothal, I felt certain she would never find someone to offer her his protection."

"You underestimate your daughter if you thought that. Any man would consider himself the most fortunate of men to have her at his side."

Rose could only stare at her husband, wondering if he was speaking from the heart or only trying to put her mother's mind at ease. He did seem to enjoy her company, however, and he'd told her he wasn't planning to deposit her here and leave. Perhaps he did care for her.

More likely she was allowing her imagination to run away with her.

"We're here, Mama, because Brantford is helping Papa. He confessed because our safety was threatened. Brantford might be able to clear his name if he can discover evidence showing that it wasn't Papa who was selling secrets to the French."

Her mother's eyes widened as Rose spoke, and she turned to Brantford. "Is that true? Can you prove his innocence?"

If she suspected her husband wasn't being entirely truthful about how he saw her to put her mother's mind at ease, his next words made it clear that wasn't the case. Brantford wasn't making any promises about the outcome of their current task just to soothe their sensibilities.

"I am hoping to discover the truth, nothing more. Your husband confessed to treason, but I have reason to believe he didn't knowingly pass on information that

SUZANNA MEDEIROS

would harm England. He tells me he has correspondence at your estate that might help to prove it. We'll be
heading there next, but first he told me that you have his
journal."

This was the first Rose was hearing about a journal,
and she felt a little pang of betrayal that he hadn't told
her the real reason for wanting to speak to her mother.
But she shouldn't have been surprised to learn he was
keeping things from her. Brantford operated under a
cloud of secrecy, after all.

"I do," Lady Worthington said. "I don't know if it
will help, but you're welcome to it."

Brantford raised a brow. "You didn't read it?"

Her mother wrung her hands together, twisting her
handkerchief. "I was afraid to. This whole situation is so
upsetting, but Rose's father insisted I take it with me
when I left London." She turned to look at Rose. "I
know you didn't approve of my leaving, but you must
know that your father insisted. He was worried about
the attention we'd receive, yes, but he also didn't want
his journal to fall into the wrong hands."

"Oh, Mama," Rose said, her heart breaking all over
again at the devastation written on her mother's face.

Her mother took a shuddering breath before continuing. "I'll admit, I was afraid it contained evidence
about his crimes, which is why I didn't want to read it. I
didn't want to believe he was capable of betraying
England. I…" She hesitated briefly. "I wanted to burn
it, but he insisted that I keep it safe. The only reason I
didn't destroy it was the knowledge that your father

couldn't possibly be in a worse position even if the authorities found it. He's already headed for the gallows," she finished with a sob.

Rose threw her arms around her mother, struggling not to break down herself.

"I think the opposite must be true. Since Papa has already confessed, he would have nothing to gain by telling Brantford about his journal. It just might contain information that will help to set him free." Rose wanted to believe that. She *had* to believe it.

"Your daughter is correct," Brantford said. "Lord Worthington would have nothing to gain by sending me on a false search for information to clear him. You should know he is very concerned about your safety. Despite his attempt to shield you, the only way to ensure the two of you come to no harm will be to apprehend the person who committed the crime to which he confessed. I'm hoping that his journal, together with the information he's hidden at your estate, will serve that purpose."

Lady Worthington cupped her daughter's face, giving her a watery smile for several seconds before turning to face Brantford. "I will help you in whatever way I can. I'll fetch the journal now. But first you must promise me that you will keep my daughter safe."

"You have my word," Brantford said without a moment's hesitation.

Rose turned to look at him and was taken aback by the intensity in her husband's gaze. In that moment, she could almost believe he cared for her.

AFTER BEING INTRODUCED to Rose's aunt and uncle, Brantford took his leave of them and followed Lady Worthington to fetch her husband's journal. He and Rose had already decided they wouldn't share the real reason for their visit with the rest of her family. As far as Lord and Lady Hayes knew, they were there for a brief visit before continuing on to Brantford's estate in Surrey. He'd already extracted Lady Worthington's promise to say nothing to her sister and brother-in-law about the matter.

He only had to wait outside Lady Worthington's bedroom a short time before she exited and handed him a small wooden box. She said nothing more, but the expression on her face told him she was afraid to hope the journal it contained could lead to the end of the nightmare for her family.

He thanked her and followed a footman to the room he and Rose would be sharing that night. After closing the door behind him, he took in the room. It wasn't particularly ornate—no doubt Lady Hayes had reserved the best guest room for her sister. Still, it was more luxurious than the inns they'd be resting at during their trip to the Worthington estate in Norfolk.

He was powerless to keep from staring at the bed, envisioning what would happen later when his wife joined him. They'd been married four days and had made love twice in a carriage and only once in a bed. He planned to take care of that discrepancy later.

Turning away, he forced himself to concentrate on the task at hand. When he lifted the lid of the plain box Lady Worthington had given him, he found a leather-bound journal within. He settled into a chair and began to read.

The journal was slim, and when he turned to the first page, he discovered that Worthington had only begun writing down his thoughts after the situation with Standish was well underway. Worthington wrote about how he'd managed to finance a season for Rose and that he'd been shocked upon arriving in London to discover he had more funds than he knew he possessed in his bank account. He then went on to detail a visit from Lord Standish later that same day, recounting his horror when the man had thanked him for sharing some information about the movements of the British fleet.

Brantford knew that Worthington had been in the navy when he was a youth and that Rose's father was still good friends with Admiral Heddington. The admiral was known for his strategic mind, but it was no secret that the man thought better when he spoke aloud. He had a few colleagues whom he trusted to keep silent after those strategy sessions, and apparently Worthington was one of them.

When Standish informed him that he had sold the information Worthington had unwittingly passed on while intoxicated, and that he'd deposited funds into Worthington's account in payment, Rose's father had been horrified. He'd tried to return the money, but Standish had already made arrangements to block any deposits to his own bank accounts that came from Worthington. And of course the man hadn't wanted to call in a third party to complete the transaction on his behalf since he hadn't wanted anyone to know his shame.

As Rose's father outlined how he'd kept the money separate from his own funds while he tried to decide what to do next, Standish had begun to hound the man for more information. When he couldn't coerce Worthington with the promise of more money, he began to threaten his wife and daughter.

As the entries continued, it was clear Worthington was becoming more distraught as the weeks passed. He kept outlining all sorts of outlandish ways in which to extricate himself from the mess he'd unwittingly embroiled himself in. The final entry was only a few lines long, stating that he had failed his family and that to keep them safe, he had to sacrifice his own life and their reputations. He took a small measure of comfort from the fact that Rose was now betrothed to Kerrick and hoped that as his countess, she would be safe.

Brantford forced himself to relax his jaw while reading that last bit. He knew Kerrick and Rose had been forced into a compromising position by Standish, who'd had designs on the man's current betrothed. Still, it bothered him more than a little to think that Rose had come very close to marrying someone else.

He flipped back over the pages but looked up when Rose entered the bedroom. He set the volume aside and watched in silence as she closed the door firmly behind her. When she turned to face him, her brows were drawn together in a frown. He stood and braced himself for the accusations he knew were coming.

"Why didn't you tell me about my father's journal?"

While he'd been expecting the question, he hadn't expected his own reaction to the hurt he could see in her eyes. "I didn't think you needed to know."

She flinched as though he'd struck her. "I see," she said. "Is there anything else you're keeping from me?"

He didn't reply. He didn't need to.

She sighed. "Of course there is."

"You asked for my assistance, Rose, and I am providing it to the best of my abilities. But there are things I cannot share with you."

She looked away, and he waited for her anger or for her demands that he allow her to read the journal.

"I apologize for my overreaction."

He was caught unaware, something that never happened to him. "You're not angry?"

"No, of course not. I won't lie and say that I'm not disappointed, but I understand. And I trust you."

Something shifted in the vicinity of his chest, unsettling him more than a little.

"I'm not even going to ask to read my father's journal. We'll just pretend that I don't already know you'd deny that request."

He didn't reply, and this time it wasn't because he was playing one of his games. He honestly didn't know what to say. His wife's trust humbled him. Instead, he opened his arms and she walked into his embrace. They stood like that for almost a full minute, words jamming in his throat as he considered what to say.

"I'm going to assume we won't need a maid or valet tonight to undress?" she said when she pulled back to look up at him. Her attempt at an innocent expression had him laughing in response.

CHAPTER 19

THEY MADE THE TRIP TO NORFOLK in a more leisurely manner over two days. Brantford restrained himself from taking his wife again in the carriage, but it was difficult to resist her temptations. It became something of a game between them, with Rose attempting to draw him from his naturally reserved manner throughout the trip. But in the end, he held out until they settled into an inn for the evening. Not because he had anything against the activity, of course. He resisted because he felt the need to keep himself from falling even further under Rose's spell.

His growing feelings for his wife were something of a mystery to him. He couldn't deny he'd been attracted to Rose Hardwick from the start, but she was quite a few years younger than him. He'd never imagined he'd find himself married to the young woman who drew men to her like bees to honey.

And yet when it became clear she was in greater

danger than he'd originally imagined, he'd had no misgivings about giving her the protection of his name.

He could no longer maintain the pretense that his actions had stemmed solely from a sense of practicality. No, by that point he'd wanted Rose for himself. Even more of a mystery was the fact that he wasn't bothered by what he would have formerly considered a weakness.

When they finally neared their destination on the second day, he arranged for the carriage to stop at the neighboring small village instead of going on to the estate.

His reasons for doing so instead of proceeding to Rose's former home were twofold, but he hadn't mentioned his intention to avoid the Worthington estate to his wife. First, he didn't know what was waiting for them at her family's home and he wanted to ensure it was safe before he allowed her to set foot in the house. He had no way of knowing what Standish might have arranged for the arrival of any of the family members.

His second reason for wanting to stay at this particular inn was the fact that it was frequented by the locals. Rose's father had run into Standish here and then proceeded to drink too much and spill the secrets that had set them all on this path. Brantford needed to speak to the innkeeper to learn what he remembered of that night. He also hoped to make a few discreet inquiries of the locals.

Rose waited until they were shown to their room before asking, "Is there a reason we're not staying at the house?"

He'd never been one to explain his actions, but at that moment he wanted to do just that. He had to resist the temptation to tell her too much.

"We'll make our way there tomorrow. I need to speak to the innkeeper while we're here. He knows your father and might have information I need."

"You could have returned to the inn to do that after we were settled at home."

He took her hands in his. "I didn't want to let you out of my sight."

Rose's eyes softened, her mouth lifting in a smile. "I feel the same. But we'll be apart if you're going to spend the evening downstairs. No doubt you'll be lurking in a dark corner, watching all the comings and goings. And before long, someone will tell you everything about what's been happening in the village and the surrounding area."

Her observation surprised him. "How is it you know me so well?"

"I probably shouldn't confess this, but during all those balls and routs, when I was doing my part to appear eager for all the attention I was receiving from others, more often than not I was watching you."

"It appears we were both doing the same thing then. Although in my case I suppose I was attempting to appear bored with all the attention. Not that I had to try very hard."

Her smile faltered as a thought occurred to her. "Do you think when you go downstairs that there will be gossip about my family?"

"Probably. But that might be overshadowed if they've seen our wedding announcement."

"You did that? Given the scandal attached to my family…"

When she didn't finish her sentence, he completed it for her. "You thought I'd want to hide the connection." He gave his head a shake. "I placed the announcement in all the papers. I want the whole world to know we're married."

"The whole world or just Lord Standish?"

Her doubt bothered him more than a little. "Everyone, Rose."

When he drew her into his arms, she rested her head on his chest. "I shouldn't say this, but I feel fortunate to have you. Given what my parents are going through, I feel like a traitor to my family for admitting that."

Brantford pulled back and tilted her chin up so she could meet his gaze. He hated the sadness he saw reflected in her blue eyes. "There will always be bad things happening in this world. Unfortunately, some of them will touch those we care about. But life would be a sad thing indeed if we didn't try to hold on to whatever happiness we could each and every moment. Never feel guilty for that."

She tilted her head to the side and examined him for several seconds. "Are you happy?"

"You can doubt that?"

She lifted a shoulder in a small shrug. "You're very good at hiding your emotions."

He brushed a thumb over her lower lip and smiled.

"I'm happy. Never question that. I hate what you are going through right now, but I can't regret that it brought us together."

ROSE WAS TIRED OF WAITING. After having dinner sent to their room, she had to wait there, alone, while Brantford went downstairs to gather what information he could.

She hadn't argued with him, but she wasn't happy about spending another day away from home. Especially since her husband had told her that their carriage driver and several of the outriders who had accompanied them on their journey were occupying all the rooms in the small inn. She had no doubt they would all come barging into the room at the slightest indication of distress on her part and could just as easily be doing the same thing at her family's estate. The servants would also be present to ensure her safety.

She hated being idle, but he'd told her the delay was only for the one night and that they would depart for her home the next day and then they could search out whatever information her father had hidden there.

But when the morning came, Brantford received a message that had him changing their plans.

"Stay here," he said. "Breakfast is already on the way up. Someone will bring all your meals up to you if I don't return soon."

With a distracted kiss, he hurried from the room.

After locking the door behind him, she began to

pace. She wished Ellen had come with them. At least her sister-in-law would have been able to keep her company as the hours passed. She might even have been able to talk Ellen into going with her to her family's estate without Brantford.

Rose stopped pacing as soon as that thought entered her mind. There was no reason why she couldn't go on ahead without Brantford. He'd told her to stay at the inn, but there wasn't any danger. Standish was in London, after all, and had no reason to follow them to Norfolk. They'd left word with the staff that they were heading to Brantford's estate in Surrey, and her husband had asked Ellen to spread the news. By now everyone in London would know about their supposed plans.

She considered asking the carriage driver to take her, but she had no way of knowing if Brantford was traveling on horseback or if he'd taken the carriage. In addition, she wouldn't be surprised if he'd told his men that she wasn't allowed to leave the room.

She was still debating the matter a few minutes later when a knock sounded at the door. She opened it to find a servant with her breakfast tray. One of her husband's men stood behind the young woman. His eyes never strayed from the servant, and he acted as though he expected her to grab the butter knife and try to stab Rose right in front of him.

She barely refrained from rolling her eyes at the man's overzealousness. She knew in that moment that no one would accompany her that day. If they even suspected she wanted to leave, she had no doubt they'd take turns standing guard outside her room.

She thanked the woman, who was more than a little unnerved by the man watching her every move, and closed the door. She pressed her ear against it, waiting to see if he would remain in the hallway, but after a minute passed she heard the heavy tread of his footsteps walking away. The sound of a door opening and closing had her releasing the breath she'd been holding.

So that meant she didn't have a guard stationed outside her room. If she was very quiet, she might be able to sneak away from the inn and make her way to her family's estate. Once there, she'd be safe with the servants present.

Since it would take her the better part of an hour to walk there, Rose sat down to eat her breakfast. There was no point in having it go to waste.

She took some time deciding what to wear. Pulling one of Brantford's coats from the trunk that had been deposited in their room, she shrugged into it and went to stand in front of the looking glass.

She looked ridiculous. No one would ever believe she was a man. Sighing, Rose returned the garment to the trunk and chose a pale yellow dress she hoped wouldn't bring too much attention to herself. She took care to scrape her hair into a severe bun. As she did so, she wished again that Brantford's sister were there. Ellen was quite skilled with makeup and would have been able to make her look older. She searched through her belongings and found a plain fichu that she could use to tie around her hair. She also made sure to remove her jewelry. After taking off her earrings and the gold necklace she wore daily, she looked down at her wedding ring and hesitated.

The stone was light blue in color and reminded Rose of her husband's eyes. It was silly, but she felt almost superstitious about removing it, so instead she turned it around so the stone would be hidden if she closed her hand.

When she was done, she scrutinized herself in the mirror. If she kept her head down and her shoulders bowed, she might pass for a servant. This whole endeavor would have been much easier if she could don a cloak, but since it was almost summer, she'd only draw more attention to herself if she wore such a heavy garment.

She'd have to move quickly and hope that none of her husband's men heard her departing. But first she had to convince them that she had no intention of leaving the room.

She opened the door and set the tray of dishes, complete with the uneaten portion of her husband's breakfast, out in the hallway. After placing the tray on the floor with an audible jangle of sound from the crockery, she stood back, hidden in her doorway. As she'd suspected, several of the doors opened immediately, and she made sure to close and lock her door with as much noise as possible. Heavens, were the men all sitting next to their own doors? If so, she'd have to be careful.

She waited several minutes, hoping all the doors had been closed. If one of the men had left the door to his room open, she'd never be able to sneak past them as her room was at the end of the hall.

Finally she decided she'd just have to brave it. She'd only get one attempt at this. If Brantford's men saw her trying to leave the inn, she wouldn't get another opportunity.

Holding her breath, she slowly opened the door and waited, thankful the hinges didn't squeak. Nothing happened. Feeling more than a little ridiculous, she closed the door with exaggerated care and made her way down the hallway at a slow, even pace. With every step she expected a floorboard to creak or a door to be thrown open, but she reached the top of the stairs without being discovered. She anticipated finding someone stationed at the bottom of the stairs, but she reached the main floor without being stopped.

Her heart was racing now, and she had the sudden realization that she was acting like a heroine in a horrid novel. For a moment she considered turning around, but she pushed back her doubts. This was real life, not fiction. She was only going home, and once there she'd be safe. After she arrived, she'd have a footman deliver a note so Brantford wouldn't worry when he returned.

Her pace quickened as she left the inn, shoulders hunched, and she turned toward her family's estate. She passed a few of the villagers, but no one paid her any attention.

With every step, she expected to hear footsteps

chasing her, but of course nothing of the sort happened. She let out a sigh of relief when, fifty minutes later, she finally reached the house.

She took a moment to compose herself, removing the fichu from her hair and tucking it away. The servants would be surprised to see her and they'd wonder why she was arriving on foot, but they wouldn't question her. Perhaps they'd heard about what happened to her father? She pushed back the thought. Servants gossiped and if they'd heard, then of course they'd have discussed it among themselves. As long as she didn't receive any pitying looks, she could pretend that nothing was amiss.

She pushed open the door and waited for the butler or one of the footmen to investigate the new arrival. When no one appeared, she moved down the hallway toward her father's study. Every second she expected to run across someone, but there was no movement, no sound. The hairs on the back of her neck rose, and for the first time she questioned the wisdom of coming here alone.

But she was already standing outside her father's study. She wouldn't examine the whole house on her own, she'd just have a quick look inside her father's study and then return to the inn.

Besides, if one of the men had discovered she'd left, it was likely someone was already on the way there. It would be fine.

CHAPTER 20

S HE KNEW WHERE TO SEARCH only because
Brantford had asked her about the layout of
the house. She'd wondered if her father had another
hidden location under the floorboards in the library or
in another room, but Brantford had wanted to know
about her father's study.

She tried to shake off her unease, telling herself she
wasn't alone in the house. The servants hadn't been
expecting her arrival, so they were probably busy doing
something else.

Brantford had told her mother that Papa had correspondence he needed to see. He hadn't said anything to
her about what he expected those letters to contain, and
it would have been pointless to ask him. She'd have to
read the letters herself to learn what they contained.

She'd ask for her husband's forgiveness later. If there
was one thing she'd learned, it was easier to ask for

absolution than for permission. Especially when it was clear that permission wouldn't be granted.

As she opened the door to her father's study, a sense of gloom settled over her. She didn't think she'd ever been in this room when her father wasn't present, and it occurred to her that he might never return.

Ignoring her unease, she walked toward the windows and drew back the curtains, hoping the clear light of day would dispel the darkness and help her to shake off her negative thoughts.

She opened a window for good measure, taking in a deep breath of the fresh air outside before turning to face her father's desk. She hesitated only for a moment before bending to open the bottom drawer on the right.

Brantford hadn't told her where to look—neither had her father—but she'd recalled the morning before they left for London. She'd walked into her father's study with a message from her mother, and he'd almost jumped out of his skin at her interruption. She'd apologized for surprising him, but he hadn't acknowledged the fright she'd given him. Instead, he'd gathered a small sheaf of papers and deposited them in that bottom drawer. Now that she thought about it, they could have been correspondence.

Hands shaking, she opened that drawer now. The papers inside were just as he'd hastily placed them all those months before. She took them out, surprised there were only a few sheets, and stared down at them. The first one was a letter from Admiral Heddington, an old friend of her father's whom she'd met several times over the years. Her eyes scanned down the page, curiosity taking hold.

"Catherine was supposed to be mine."

Rose jumped, her heart in her throat at the unexpected voice. When she looked up, Lord Standish stood just inside the doorway, his dark hair unkempt in a way she'd never seen it. He'd always struck her as being fastidious about his appearance. But worse were his eyes. His tone had seemed casual, but something in the way his eyes were narrowed—trained on her with unrelenting focus—told her that he was anything but calm. She moved her hands behind her back, hoping he hadn't taken note of the pages she was now gripping tightly.

She straightened her shoulders and tried her best not to betray just how much his presence unnerved her. "Lord Standish, what are you doing here?"

He tsked. "Come now, don't tell me you weren't expecting me. Or perhaps you were expecting someone else. A certain fair-haired gentleman?"

She tried to ignore the sneer in his voice, but her own was not quite steady when she replied. "It is highly improper for you to be alone with me. You will have to leave."

"Are you going to make me?"

The look he gave her warned her that she just might not come out of this encounter with her life. Still, she had to try.

She moved closer to the bellpull hidden behind the curtain. "I won't have to," she said, giving it a sharp yank with one hand. "The butler will be here momentarily."

He laughed and moved farther into the room. "You're going to have to try harder if you expect me to believe your lies. I can see your heart racing from here. And we both know the house is empty. I made certain to send word, in your name, of course, giving the staff the day off. Those who chose to stay behind... Well, they won't be interrupting us."

She tried not to think about what Standish might have done. The man was clearly insane. She couldn't help remembering the evening she and Brantford had consummated their marriage. How he'd stormed into her room, his concern for her safety very real. Why hadn't she heeded his warning not to leave the inn?

Fear hollowed out her stomach, and her hands began to shake. "My husband—"

"—received some information that took him elsewhere, so it is just the two of us."

He smiled then, and a frisson of ice slithered down her spine.

"I don't know what you want from me."

"Don't you? If you hadn't ended your betrothal with that self-important blighter, Catherine would have been mine by now. You are a poor replacement, especially now that you've allowed yourself to be sullied, but I suppose you will have to do. When I'm finished, I expect you to thank me and then hand me the papers you're trying to hide behind your back. And if you're a good girl, I might make your death quick."

She struggled to keep her rising panic at bay as she ran through the exits in the room. Brantford had told her that Lord Standish was dangerous, but she hadn't truly believed he was capable of murder.

Standish stood between her and the door, and there was no way she could reach it without him intercepting her. She recalled then the window she had opened. If she created a distraction, she might be able to escape through it. She'd opened it quite wide, and her father's study was on the main floor. Standish was much larger than her. If he couldn't follow, he'd have to exit through the main door. She knew she wouldn't be able to outrun him, but those few precious seconds might give her the opportunity to hide somewhere on the estate.

She didn't like her chances of success, but she couldn't just stand there and do nothing. She had to at least try to escape.

She began to edge toward the door, and as expected, Standish moved to intercept. Moving quickly, she overturned a small table, hoping it would buy her enough time, and turned to the right. The open window was only a few steps away and her hand was on the sill, the pages still clutched within her grasp, one leg poised to climb out, when two arms captured her about the waist. Panic streaked through her, and she cried out in fear as she tried to claw at his hands, scattering the pages around them. Her ineffectual attempt to escape only seemed to amuse him.

His laughter, tinged with more than a slight hint of madness, had her twisting in his grasp and attempting to bite his arm. His amusement didn't end, but he spun her around and raised a hand to strike her. She closed her eyes and braced herself for the blow, but it never came.

He released her suddenly and she stumbled, opening her eyes to see Brantford struggling with Lord Standish. Her heart almost stopped when she saw the latter raise a pistol, but before she could call out a warning her husband had disarmed the man in a series of moves that left her jaw hanging open. He'd told her once when she'd expressed concern over his own safety that he was proficient in some form of Eastern self-defense, but watching the ease with which he disabled the other man shocked her.

Standish was lying facedown on the floor, breathing heavily and no longer laughing. Brantford held the man's arms in an iron grip and leaned into him, a knee pressed into his back. Her husband jerked Standish's arms upward, eliciting a sharp grunt before turning to face her.

"Did he hurt you?"

"No," she said, realizing only then that she was shaking. "You arrived in time."

His eyes moved over her as though he was trying to convince himself of the truth of her words before he turned, again, to look down at the man he'd so easily incapacitated.

"If you could give me something to bind him…"

Standish started laughing again, and despite the fact that he was no longer a danger to her, Rose couldn't stop the shiver that went through her at the maniacal sound.

"I didn't really want her anyway. She's used goods… You can have her."

Heat rose in her cheeks as she turned away to find something, anything, that Brantford could use to secure the man who'd bragged about doing unspeakable things to her. Her eyes moved to the curtains, but she remembered that her father's study didn't have decorative cording to tie them back. A flurry of movement had her turning back toward the pair in time to see that Brantford had rolled Standish over and smashed his fist into the man's face.

Standish's eyes rolled backward and silence descended.

Brantford stood then and turned to face her. "I'll still need that rope, but at least now we won't have to listen to his ravings."

With a small sound of relief, she threw herself into her husband's arms, taking comfort in the way they tightened around her.

"I didn't think you'd arrive. Standish said he'd sent you to follow another lead…"

He pulled back then and gazed down at her. He raised a hand to her face, his thumb caressing her cheek. "I sent someone else to follow that lead. I wasn't about to allow you to remain on your own. Not with your penchant for taking matters into your own hands."

Normally she would have protested that statement since she'd only done exactly what he'd asked her to do since they'd wed. If he'd suspected Standish might be present in her home, he should have told her. But she was so happy he was there—and she did have to admit that he was correct, for she hadn't told anyone she was planning to visit the estate alone—that she let the statement pass.

"He could wake up at any moment... I should go find that rope."

He dropped his hand from her face and released her, taking a step back. She mourned the loss of his arms around her, but she couldn't stop envisioning Lord Standish leaping up from his prone state and attacking them again.

CHAPTER 21

BRANTFORD WATCHED ROSE'S RETREATING FORM as she rushed from the room, his pulse still racing as he recalled the scene that had met him upon arriving at her family's estate. The house had been far too quiet, and he'd known immediately that his wife was in danger.

He hadn't thought it necessary to share the details of why he wanted to avoid the house, thinking he'd ease some of her worries by holding back his suspicion that the home in which she'd been raised might not be safe. But the only thing he'd accomplished was to leave her ripe for the picking, and Standish had wasted no time swooping in.

It had been a careless decision. He should have told her why she needed to stay away from the house. Yes, he'd told her not to leave their room, but without reason to be cautious, of course Rose wouldn't be content to remain idle.

They'd had so little time together, and he'd come so close to losing her. He hadn't allowed himself to think about their future, but in that moment he realized he wanted all of it with her. He'd never thought he would marry, but he'd come to realize that his reasons for proposing to Rose had been entirely selfish. And heaven help him, he wanted children with her and everything a life together could hold.

He approached Standish where he lay prone on the floor and nudged him a little harder than necessary with one boot. Satisfied that he wasn't pretending at being unconscious, Brantford reached for the pistol he'd kicked away when they'd struggled for the weapon. He lowered himself into a chair and waited for Rose to return.

He hoped Standish would regain consciousness before then. There was nothing he wanted more than to smash his fist into the other man's face again. Barely suppressed anger bubbled up within him as he recalled the sight that had greeted him when he'd followed the sound of maniacal laughter to the library. His heart had almost frozen when he'd heard Rose cry out, and a black rage had engulfed him when he saw Standish raise a hand to strike her. It had taken every ounce of willpower he possessed not to kill the man with his bare hands.

Rose returned several minutes later, a hank of rope that she'd found somewhere dangling from one hand. She must have run the whole way, for her breath was coming in quick little pants. Despite what everyone thought, Brantford was human. He couldn't keep his eyes from dropping down to take in the sight of her breasts rising and falling, remembering other, more pleasant times she'd been short of breath.

He ruthlessly tamped down those memories. There would be time for that later, but right then it was clear that Rose was still very shaken by her recent ordeal. To be honest, his nerves weren't entirely steady either.

She hesitated in the doorway, nervous about coming too close to Standish.

He rose and crossed the room to take the rope from her. "Keep this safe," he said, handing her the pistol before turning to secure Standish's arms and legs. He might have handled the man more roughly than was necessary, but no one would fault him. He already knew Standish was headed for the hangman's noose. Given what he knew was in the correspondence Worthington had received from Admiral Heddington, nothing would save Standish now. Even if he didn't hang for treason, Brantford would make sure he paid for the murder of his cousin and a good number of young women in France.

But he'd dealt with men like Standish before, and knew how to make them talk. With Standish having been foiled in the end, Brantford knew the man would take pleasure in sharing just how easily he'd duped Worthington. Brantford counted on that hubris, for it was the only thing that would save Rose's father.

For good measure, Brantford stuffed his handkerchief into the man's mouth. He couldn't guarantee he wouldn't kill the man otherwise if he started disparaging his wife again.

He turned his back on Standish and led Rose outside, making sure to take the pistol from her first. She clung to his arm without speaking.

His carriage was making its way down the driveway. When he'd returned to the inn and seen that Rose wasn't there, he'd known immediately where to find her. He'd left instructions for the carriage to be driven to the house but had made his own way on horseback. He couldn't allow himself to think about what might have happened if he'd arrived even a few minutes later.

When the carriage stopped, he instructed the driver to take Standish into his custody and make arrangements to transport him to London.

Normally he would have traveled with them, but he knew Standish would be secure in the more-than-capable hands of his driver. They'd worked together for years, and the man possessed skills that rivaled his own. No, he had to stay with Rose, who needed him more right now. That he didn't want to be away from her either was a given.

"I can't go back inside the house right now. I think I'll need a few days before I'll feel safe here again."

Her voice was devoid of emotion, her expression blank, and Brantford knew she was in shock.

He led her to the side of the house where he'd hastily tethered his horse when no groom came out to greet him. He and Rose would ride back to the inn together.

The tentative control he'd held over his emotions when he realized Standish had Rose in his clutches—the notorious reserve for which he was famous—was threatening to unravel. He needed to hold Rose close and ensure nothing bad would ever happen to her again.

CHAPTER 22

*J*UST TWO SHORT HOURS EARLIER, Rose couldn't have imagined how relieved she'd be to return to the inn. She and Brantford hadn't spoken as they rode back at a slow pace. He must have sensed that she needed that extra time to compose herself.

She sat sideways in front of him on the gelding, her arms wrapped about his waist. Burying her face against his shoulder, she tried to draw some of her husband's strength into herself. Try as she might, she couldn't stop her thoughts from circling back to what might have happened had he not arrived in time, picturing all too well what Standish had wanted to do to her.

When they finally arrived at the inn, he slid from the horse's back and lifted her down. They stood like that for several seconds, his hands on her waist, hers on his shoulders. Staring up into his face, she was barely aware of the groom approaching to take care of their mount.

She could see the tumult of emotion in Brantford's eyes as he gazed down at her and she braced herself, expecting to be chastised for her reckless behavior. It was what she deserved, after all. She never should have thought she knew their situation better than he.

She opened her mouth to offer an apology, but he gave a small shake of his head. Grasping her hand, he led her into the inn without a word.

When they reached their room, she wasn't surprised to see one of his men stationed outside the door. What's more, she was actually happy to see him there. His presence meant Standish hadn't escaped and that he wasn't hiding in their room, waiting for them. She wondered how long it would take for her to stop expecting him to jump out at her from the shadows.

The burly man stepped aside, and Brantford led them into the room. She wanted to cling to him again, but he hadn't closed the door.

"I need to apprise the men about what has happened. I'll only be a few minutes. Lock this door behind me."

Rose nodded as she struggled with the urge to beg him not to leave. This was what Brantford did, after all. Given how quickly he had taken Standish down, it was apparent that he dealt with such men all the time. Why else would he be so skilled in physical combat?

She locked the door as soon as he closed it, then turned to stare at the sparse room. Feeling silly given the fact that their room was now being guarded, she nonetheless moved to look behind the screen that set off a small dressing area in the corner of the room. Then she bent to look underneath the bed. Finally, squaring her shoulders, she yanked open the wardrobe door. It was blessedly empty save for the few garments a maid had hung up the day before.

Sagging, she moved to sit on the edge of the bed. It was only then that she realized she was shaking. Closing her eyes, she took several deep breaths as she tried to think of the good that would come of this. If Brantford could get a confession from Standish, it was possible her father would soon be free. She pictured that reunion, imagining the joy her parents would feel at finally being able to resume their lives. Hopefully, once everyone learned that her father had only confessed to protect his family, they'd finally be allowed back into society. She knew how much it meant to her mother to be able to hold her head high while among her peers.

The fact that Rose had married the elusive Earl of Brantford would probably go a long way toward achieving that end. As for Rose, she would never forgive all those who had turned their back on her family in their hour of need. But at least she had Catherine and, by extension, her family. They had been nothing but kind and supportive to her.

A quick knock at the door surprised her. When she heard Brantford's voice announcing it was him, she flew across the room and unlocked the door. She waited only until he closed the door behind him before throwing herself into his arms.

The tears came then, much as she tried to hold them

back. Brantford wouldn't appreciate a weepy wife, but she couldn't seem to stop.

The world shifted, and she realized he was carrying her to the bed. He sat, holding her in his lap, and her tears only increased.

"Shh," he said, stroking her hair. "You've had a shock. Let it all out. Everything will be fine now." His other arm tightened around her waist as she tried to burrow farther into him.

When her crying finally slowed, she pulled back and gazed up at her husband. She should have been embarrassed about losing control so completely, especially in front of him, but instead all she could feel was a sense of wonder as she saw the concern in Brantford's eyes.

"I expected you to box my ears for going against your instructions. Instead, I find this mysteriously compassionate man has taken possession of my husband's body."

A corner of his mouth lifted at her attempt at humor, but it was gone almost as soon as it appeared. "I am equal parts torn between turning you over my knee and giving you a lesson you won't soon forget or holding you close and never letting go of you again."

"If I'm to have a choice in the matter, I'd prefer the latter."

He cupped her face, his thumb stroking against her lower lip, and a shiver of awareness went through her. "You frightened me half to death today."

"Only half? My heart almost stopped when Lord Standish grabbed me. If you hadn't been there…" A shudder wracked her body. "How did you know I was there? You were going somewhere else."

"That's what Standish intended," Brantford replied, his eyes narrowing a fraction. "But I've always been a firm believer in trusting my instincts, and something didn't seem right. I sent someone in my stead and came back to make sure you were safe. Imagine my surprise when I discovered you were gone."

She winced at the censure in his voice. "In my defense, I never imagined the house would be empty. I still don't know how he emptied it of all the servants." She hesitated as she remembered the glee in Lord Standish's voice when he'd mentioned that they wouldn't be interrupted. "Do you think he hurt them?"

"Some of my men are on the way right now. I imagine he did nothing more than restrain them and lock them in a room."

She wanted to believe that was true. "How did you know I'd gone to the house?"

"Where else would you have gone? There was no sign of a struggle here, and despite the ease with which you seem to have slipped away, I like to think that at least one of the men would have noticed if you'd been dragged off." His jaw tightened as he struggled with his emotions. "I'll confess I was worried that you'd been waylaid somewhere en route. And when I realized you were in the study with Standish…" He gave his head a sharp shake. "I don't know how I didn't kill him for laying his hands on you. If he'd gone further—"

She placed a hand over his mouth to stop him. "He

didn't. You arrived in time, thank heaven." Her heart was so full at that moment, she couldn't stop the next words that tumbled from her lips. "I love you, Lucien. I've loved you since before we were married. I never imagined then that my ill-conceived infatuation would lead to our being married. And even if you don't love me in return—"

He took her mouth in a short but thorough kiss before pulling back. "I was jealous of Kerrick when he was courting you, even though I knew he really cared for Catherine."

"What?" She must have misheard him. "You scarce knew I existed. If you weren't investigating my father's activities, you wouldn't have even known I was alive."

"Never doubt that I noticed you. Every man with a set of eyes has noticed you."

"Lucien," she said with a mock frown. "Why did you go through that whole charade of asking Kerrick to court me? Poor Catherine was so heartbroken."

"Because, my dear temptress, I wanted you too much. Which meant I had to keep you at a distance."

"Of course," she said with a wry twist of her lips. "Heaven forbid the Unaffected Earl admit his attraction to a woman."

"Oh, I've been attracted to plenty of women, but none of them ever posed a danger to my heart."

Her breath caught and she barely managed her next words. "What are you saying?"

He cupped the back of her head with one hand and

used the other to bring her flush against him. "I'm saying that I love you too."

Tears threatened to spill at his confession. Even though she'd come to suspect that he cared for her, she'd never imagined he would ever admit as much. There was so much she wanted to say, so much she wanted to ask. But that would have to wait until later because Brantford kissed her then, and she never wanted him to stop.

EPILOGUE

July 1807

*A*FTER HER MAID PINNED THE LAST CURL IN PLACE, Rose left her bedroom and rushed to join her husband downstairs.

Brantford had done it. Lord Standish had confessed to being the mastermind behind the scheme to frame her father for treason, and now Papa was free. Her parents had arrived at their estate in Surrey earlier that day and were resting before coming down for dinner.

Brantford had found the evidence that Standish had been selling secrets to the French for some time locked away at the man's estate. Faced with the knowledge that he'd soon be hanged for his crimes, he'd taken one final swipe at her father. She'd feared he would remain mute and that she'd also see her father hanged, but apparently Standish's pride had him revealing his whole scheme. How he'd tricked her father into spilling what he knew about the movements of the Royal Navy by getting him thoroughly foxed first. And how he'd deposited money into her father's bank account to make it appear as though he were complicit in the entire scheme.

Her father's reputation had taken a blow when the details came out, but better to be thought foolish and easily misled than to be branded a traitor.

Rose hurried into the drawing room, relieved when she saw she'd made it downstairs before her parents. Her husband, of course, was as immaculate as ever, dressed in dark colors, every strand of fair hair lying exactly where it should. He put down the book he was reading and stood, greeting her with a quick kiss.

"I can scarce believe we have finally arrived at this point. Not that I doubted you, Lucien, but it seemed too much to hope for."

"I haven't quite forgiven your father for putting all of you in danger in the first place."

Rose brushed off the criticism. It wasn't the first time she'd heard it, and she knew it wouldn't be the last.

"We never would have wed otherwise since you were so determined to ignore me. I'm not sure if I should forgive you either for that. I spent many a night pining after the handsome earl who never glanced my way."

Brantford made a soft sound that made it clear he didn't believe her. "I'm amazed you could see me beyond the crowd of men surrounding you."

She tilted her head, amused that he still seemed so annoyed about her popularity during the past season. "It wasn't their attention I wanted."

"You did nothing to forestall it."

"Yes, well, I probably shouldn't admit this, but I was trying to make you notice me. I thought that perhaps curiosity would have you seeking to at least speak to me. But you never did."

"No, and I can admit now that I was a fool. When I think that someone else could have captured your attention—"

"It never would have happened."

He pulled her into his arms and smiled down at her. "I'm going to have to be extra vigilant in future."

Rose's brows drew together. "Why? I know you told me about that silly bet people are placing about who can lure me from your side, but you should know that you're the only man I want."

Brantford shook his head. "Not that. I trust you. Also, I have no problem hurting anyone who tries to get to close to you. No, I'm afraid my reputation is now at risk."

Rose drew back, hurt at what her husband had revealed. "You're ashamed to be seen with me?"

"No, my dear. I'm worried that everyone will see how decidedly affected I am by your presence. Ellen has taken great joy in telling me that I look like a lovesick pup whenever you enter the room."

Rose laughed. "Ellen is just giving you a hard time. I think she feels it's her job as your sister."

"She's not entirely wrong though. I feel like a lovesick pup whenever you're around. It's quite embarrassing."

Laughing, Rose dragged her husband's head down for a quick kiss. It turned into a heated embrace quite quickly, and it was only the sound of a throat being cleared that snapped her back to the present.

Brantford stepped away, and she turned to find her parents had just entered the room. Her mother was beaming, her smile wider than Rose recalled ever having seen it.

Rose couldn't bring herself to meet her father's gaze.

"It appears I was mistaken yet again," Worthington said. "I didn't believe Rose's mother when she told me the two of you had made a love match. I'd had you pegged for a cold fish."

Brantford stiffened at the accusation, then let out a long-suffering sigh. "See what I mean, Rose? My reputation will be ruined ere long."

Rose couldn't hold back her laugh, amused at her husband's very real distress. She looked at him, then at her parents, before rushing forward to hug her father, as she'd already done numerous times since their arrival that afternoon.

She'd never imagined she could have everything she wanted, but here she was, happily married to the man she'd loved from afar and celebrating her father's release. She almost pinched herself to make sure she wasn't dreaming. When she returned to her husband's side, joy radiated through her at the fond look in his eyes, assuring her she was, indeed, quite awake.

∼

Thank you for reading *The Unaffected Earl*. If you enjoyed this book, you can share that enjoyment by recommending it to others and leaving a review.

To learn when Suzanna has a new release, you can sign up to receive an email alert at:
https://www.suzannamedeiros.com/newsletter/

To read more about the author's books and learn where you can buy copies, you can visit the "Books" page on the author's website:
https://www.suzannamedeiros.com/books/

Books 2 and 3 in the *Hathaway Heirs* series—*Lord Hathaway's New Bride* and *The Captain's Heart*—are available now. For a sneak peek, turn the page.

EXCERPT—LORD HATHAWAY'S
NEW BRIDE

THE MORNING OF JAMES HATHAWAY'S WEDDING should have been a happy one. After all, he now had everything a man could desire.

Despite his uncle's best attempts to sire a son, he had died without an heir. Upon his death, the title of Viscount Hathaway had passed to James, and with it had come a great deal of land and wealth.

He hadn't expected to inherit, and so he'd never given more than a passing thought to the title and all that would come with it before his uncle's passing. But the title had gained him the one thing he'd recently discovered he desired beyond all else—his new wife.

Her father, a baronet living near Hathaway Park in Northampton, had paid James a call when he'd taken up residence. Sir Henry Mapleton had made not-so-subtle references to his daughter during that visit, but by that point James had already become accustomed to the seemingly unending parade of mothers and fathers who made no pretense about throwing their unmarried daughters at him. Daughters whom he had no intention of courting.

Then he'd met Sarah Mapleton.

He'd done everything in his power to try to engage her regard, but she'd barely even looked at him whenever their paths crossed—and her father had taken every opportunity to ensure that happened often.

James knew she'd only accepted his suit because her father had pressed her to. He hoped that with time and patience she would come to accept him fully, but as he watched her during the wedding breakfast, it was clear to him that it would not be that day.

The wedding ceremony had been an intimate affair. From his side, there was only his mother and younger sister, his uncle's widow and the man he knew would be her husband when her official mourning period was over. He wished Edward were there, but having recently been promoted to the rank of captain in the British army, his brother was engaged on the continent.

Sarah's immediate family was equally small—her parents and a younger brother, George, who'd come down from Eton for the day. But the wedding breakfast was a different matter. They'd opened the house to friends and neighbors in Northampton, which meant that strangers, few of whom he'd even met before that morning, now flooded several rooms on the main floor of the manor.

Sarah sat next to him during the actual meal, but she'd spoken only a few words. In fact, she'd hardly

glanced at him, doing so only when he forced her attention by addressing her directly. From her demeanor
when he'd begun to court her, he'd originally thought
her shy. He'd since witnessed her several times in other
company and had come to realize that she was only
reserved with him.

Leaning against one wall of the large dining room,
he watched her flit from guest to guest, showing them
the outgoing side of her personality that she kept hidden
from him. Despite her efforts, he saw enough to realize
she was acting a part for their guests. His wife certainly
looked the picture of a beautiful, happy bride. Her silk
dress of white seemed to shimmer as she moved about
the room, her blond curls bouncing as if they, too, had
been ordered to appear happy and confident. But he
couldn't help noticing that she laughed just a little too
loudly, smiled a little too stiffly. He wondered if it was as
obvious to everyone else that his new bride would rather
be anywhere else than here, celebrating their marriage.

He also didn't miss the way one young man kept
looking at Sarah, trying to find opportunities to speak to
her, and how she went out of her way to avoid him.
Robert Vaughan. James had made it his mission to learn
his identity, and it hadn't comforted him to discover that
many had once thought he and Sarah would make a
love match.

His thoughts were diverted by yet another person
demanding his attention. Never good with names under
even the best of circumstances, James could have told
the portly older man that his effort at currying favor

while he was surrounded by so many new faces was unlikely to bear fruit.

After ten minutes of tedious conversation about politics and current happenings on the continent that served only to make him worry more about his brother, James made some vague excuse about being needed elsewhere and went in search of his wife, who had disappeared. Leaving the dining room, he made his way through the other open rooms on the main floor.

He found Sarah in the drawing room, seated on the settee next to a young woman he didn't know. His wife's posture was stiff, her brows drawn together in a slight frown. Feeling the need to rescue her, he crossed to where they sat on the far side of the room. He was almost upon the pair when the other woman's whispered words reached his ears.

"…can't believe you were actually forced to marry someone so common. He may have inherited the title, but there can be no mistaking that he doesn't come from the same noble stock as the old viscount. How can you stand it?"

He froze in place, waiting to hear his wife defend him. But instead she looked down at her hands, which were clasped tightly in her lap, and shrugged. Disappointment surged within him.

The other woman looked up then and made a strangled noise of dismay. James didn't even glance at her, all his attention focused instead on Sarah. His wife looked up at that moment to see what had alarmed her companion. Their gazes met and clashed.

"It was so nice to have a few minutes to talk to you," the woman said, stumbling over her words and rising with unseemly haste. He didn't look at her as she fled from the room.

Sarah tore her gaze from his and rose as well. He supposed he should have been angry, but given how tense things were between the two of them, he wasn't surprised. He couldn't think of anything to say that wouldn't make the situation worse, and since the room had become more crowded since he'd entered—were people actually following him?—he murmured something about wanting to introduce her to his mother and sister. She nodded, managing a small, tense smile for the benefit of those who were unabashedly watching them, and took his arm.

https://www.suzannamedeiros.com/books/series-hathaway-heirs/lord-hathaways-new-bride/

©2018 Suzanna Medeiros

EXCERPT—THE CAPTAIN'S HEART

GRACE MOVED SILENTLY THROUGH THE HOUSE and exited by means of a window in her father's study. Helen had already gone to bed, exhausted from having risen early that morning and spending hours in a carriage. That left Grace free to slip out of the house shortly after the sun went down. She couldn't risk trying to saddle a horse herself and being caught, so she set out on foot in the direction of the village.

It took her three quarters of an hour to reach the cottage the captain had mentioned he'd be renting for the remainder of his stay in Somerset. When she finally arrived, her stomach was in knots. She could very well imagine what Hathaway's servant—surely he'd have at least one with him—would think when he found an unescorted woman paying a call after dark.

She almost sagged with relief when the door was opened by Hathaway himself. Surprise, then delight, lit his face when he saw her. He glanced over her shoulder and his smile turned into a frown.

"Please tell me you didn't arrive on foot?"

She couldn't resist the urge to dip into a deep curtsy, saying, "It is very nice to see you too, Captain."

For a moment she thought he was going to lecture her about safety, but in the end, his good humor won out. He opened the door even wider, and she stepped into the hallway.

"I'd offer you refreshments, but…" He gave a small shrug. "I only have my valet with me and he has gone out."

Hathaway's words set one small part of her mind at ease. At least he didn't have scores of servants who would immediately brand her a trollop.

They were alone in the house, and her pretense was now at an end. Grace took a deep breath to steady her nerves and met his gaze. There was no point moving to the small sitting room she spied on the right. Once he learned the truth, the captain would give her Freddie's letter, and she would be on her way again.

"I am here to let you know my sister arrived this afternoon." She hesitated, dreading what she must confess now.

Hathaway nodded. "I'll call tomorrow then."

Somehow she had to tell him the truth. "About that, there is something I must tell you. I—" She froze when Hathaway placed a finger over her lips.

"Let me speak first."

The way he was looking at her, the fact that his hand

had moved and now he was cupping her face, rubbing his thumb over her lower lip, left her bereft of speech. She could only nod.

"Once my duty here is discharged, I will be leaving."

She waited, knowing he wanted to say more.

"I don't want to waste what little time we have together talking about your sister. I would much rather talk about you and me."

He stepped closer so their bodies were almost touching and she found it difficult to breathe. She could see the heat in his eyes as he gazed down at her, trying to tell her without words just what he wanted from her.

She wanted the same thing.

https://www.suzannamedeiros.com/books/series-hathaway-heirs/the-captains-heart/

©2015 Suzanna Medeiros

ABOUT THE AUTHOR

Suzanna Medeiros was born and raised in Toronto, Canada. Her love for the written word led her to pursue a degree in English Literature from the University of Toronto. She went on to earn a Bachelor of Education degree, but graduated at a time when no teaching jobs were available. After working at a number of interesting places, including a federal inquiry, a youth probation office, and the Office of the Fire Marshal of Ontario, she decided to pursue her first love—writing.

Suzanna is married to her own hero and is the proud mother of twin daughters. She is an avowed romantic who enjoys spending her days writing love stories.

She would like to thank her parents for showing her that love at first sight and happily ever after really do exist.

To learn more about Suzanna's books, you can visit her website at:
https://www.suzannamedeiros.com
or visit her on Facebook at:
https://www.facebook.com/AuthorSuzannaMedeiros

To learn when she has a new release available, you can sign up for her new release mailing list at: https://www.suzannamedeiros.com/newsletter

BOOKS BY SUZANNA MEDEIROS

Dear Stranger

Forbidden in February (A Year Without a Duke)

The Novellas: A Collection

Landing a Lord series:

Dancing with the Duke

Loving the Marquess

Beguiling the Earl

The Unaffected Earl

The Unsuitable Duke — Coming Soon

Hathaway Heirs series:

Lady Hathaway's Indecent Proposal

Lord Hathaway's New Bride

The Captain's Heart

For more information please visit the "Books" page on the
author's website:

https://www.suzannamedeiros.com/books/

Made in the USA
Monee, IL
16 June 2023

35950802R00141